The Candlelight Chapel

The Candlelight Chapel

JENNIFER GRIFFITH

The Candlelight Chapel

ISBN: 9798342273152

This is a work of fiction. Names, characters, places and events are creations of the author's imagination or are used fictitiously. Any resemblance to actual persons, living or dead, events or locations is purely coincidental.

Cover art © Blue Water Books, 2024. Stock art licensed from Depositphoto.com.

For Uncle Walt

the first Western artist I knew and admired

Chapter 1

Hazel Hollings

F alls View Chapel loomed in front of me. White clapboard, arched windows of stained glass, the steeple pointing skyward. Snow had slid from the steep roof and piled near the foundation already. Winter's depths came early to Massey Falls, making it feel Christmassy much sooner than other places, including Reedsville.

Which I'd fled in a cloud of shame.

"Anybody here?" I ventured inside, my heart pounding under the tidal wave of the past. "Aunt Gretchen?" Nothing. "Ms. Eileen?"

No response. But Ms. Eileen was *always* here. Wasn't Aunt Gretchen supposed to be waiting for me to let me into the basement apartment where I grew up?

Not everyone gets to grow up in a chapel. Well, in a chapel's basement, in my case. On account of Dad's situation, I was pretty lucky to even have a roof over my head at all. Bless him for still trying, of course. And, all things considered, it had turned out to be the very best thing for me to be right there with the musical opportunity that had been the lodestar of my life.

Well, until lately.

"Hello?" The back of my throat got that annoying tremor that came anytime I was in a highly emotional state. But I wouldn't let my eyes

1

well up. Stupid *easy-crier* curse.

A clattering sounded, metallic and hollow against a wood floor. I jogged toward the sound. It had come from the chapel. Was Ms. Eileen all right? Could she have fallen?

I pressed open the large double doors of the chapel proper. Inside, the aisles, chairs, and every pew were draped with plastic drop cloths, as was the pulpit, and ...

Whoa. My soul lurched.

As impossible as it may seem, two sights hit me simultaneously—like a one-two punch. One was the sight of the stately organ at the front of the room where I'd spent ten thousand hours of my youth playing and perfecting my skills. The other was an impressively tall young man in spattered overalls holding a dripping paint roller. He set down the roller and took off a painter's smock.

Good heavens!

He was wearing my dad's sweater.

Adrenaline surged all through me, and my head filled with fog. Who was he? Why was he wearing Dad's sweater?

He was lit from behind by the sun coming through the arched window, so I couldn't see his face. But there was zero question about the sweater. I'd made it for Dad myself, and he'd worn it every winter day of his too-short life. The sleeves barely came halfway down the man's lanky arms.

"There you are!" My aunt sailed in, her arms wide. "Come here, my dear one. I am so sorry I was on the phone with a colleague in Borneo when you arrived. I should have been up here to meet you." Aunt Gretchen enfolded me in the most motherly hug I could imagine. I returned the hug, and tears squeezed from me, as our hearts pressed together. "Oh, look at you! All grown into a gorgeous young woman."

Gorgeous? Ha. I retracted my arms instinctively, hiding my right hand even deeper within the sleeve of my coat, the ache as sharp as the day it had ceased to function. "You're the beautiful one in the family, Gretchen. How was Antarctica? I can't believe you've been to *all* the continents. Who gets to do that?"

From the side of the room, the young man coughed and then turned his head quickly. I caught his profile when he did so. It looked familiar, but I couldn't place it.

Aunt Gretchen released me and turned. "Oh, Isaac, I didn't see you there. You're doing such a nice job on the chapel. I bet Ms. Eileen is so pleased." She dragged me off without giving an introduction, but I gave a curious glance over my shoulder as we left the room. The light around him shifted, and I could see his face at last. The big, soulful blue eyes were no strangers to me, but he wasn't an Isaac.

He was *Ike*.

Ike, though? Ike Ivey? It couldn't be. I shot into a time machine to my childhood when Dad was the caretaker here at Falls View Chapel and he'd fallen and hurt himself, as he was apt to do. Ike had come along and offered to help him—without pay—if Dad would train him in a few things. He'd made it so Dad could keep his job, which meant we could stay on living at the chapel and retain access to the organ for my daily practicing.

Ike had been a hero to my family. But ... wasn't he away at medical school?

We arrived at the bottom of the stairwell that led to the basement apartment, and Aunt Gretchen flung the door open and kicked off her shoes in the foyer. "Do you like what I've done to the place?" She grinned like she knew the secret of the universe—which, if anyone did, it was Aunt Gretchen. She'd been everywhere and done everything and knew everyone. Basically, the opposite of my life up to now, and definitely the opposite of my future, thanks to the injury.

I gazed around the room at the orange- and avocado-green-striped wallpaper, the low ceiling with its brass and glass chandelier from the era before my parents went to high school, the oak cabinets, the stainless-steel sink, the harvest-gold appliances. "Forgive me, but it looks just the same, other than you put up your travel map with the pins in places you've been." Even the furniture—which had been owing to

3

Ms. Eileen Elderberry's charity for him and our situation—hadn't changed since the day Dad and I moved in.

"Yep!" Gretchen beamed. "I'd never touch a thing. It's a capsule of a better, more peaceful time. A time when shag carpet ruled the world." She bent over and touched her bare toes, which she squidged in the twists of carpet yarn. "Aren't you glad?"

"I am, honestly." Home looked and felt—mostly—like home. Not a hundred percent, what with Dad being gone. "Thanks." I fell onto the sofa, and she promptly brought us mugs of hot cocoa and a plate of graham crackers.

"I hope you still like marshmallows." She plopped beside me and curled her feet underneath her, hiding them in her bohemian-style skirt—a huge contrast to my highly conventional sweater twinset and pencil trousers. Funny, since I had the artistic career, and she was the corporate one. "So, darling niece. Give me the scoop."

I must have winced. Was I really ready to bare my soul to anyone—even Aunt Gretchen—about the tragedy of my lost career in the music world? "It's, um ..." With great focus, I pressed the fingers of my disobliging hand outward, urging them to straighten. It was no use. "You mean about why I left Reedsville?"

"Ah, not that," she said as she threw her head back and cackled, her curls boinging and her large hoop earrings clanging against each other. "I meant, what was that *en flagrante* look between you and Ike Ivey? I was glued to the floor watching the electricity between you."

"There was electricity?" I hadn't felt it. Just shock. Okay, I guess electricity does create shock. "I didn't even recognize him, and then you called him Isaac, and I got thrown off. What's he doing painting the chapel? I thought he—"

"Yeah, yeah." Gretchen waved a graham cracker segment at me. "Everyone thought he was in medical school." She rolled her eyes. "Don't bring it up with him. He's a good painter."

Okay. That made sense. I mean, he was tall enough that with an extender on the roller handle, he probably barely needed a step stool to reach the top of the wall. "That's nice." I wanted to change the topic—but to Gretchen and not me—so I asked her about Antarctica and Borneo, and she gave me an hour's worth of stories.

"You should come with me next time!" She set her empty cocoa mug on the table. She'd been using it for emphasis during her storytelling. "Oh, too bad you have that job that keeps you basically chained to the piano bench."

"Organ," I corrected, and then my conscious mind accused me. *Not anymore.* And I'm sure I flushed red, considering how flaming hot my face became. "You're staying through Christmas, I hope?"

Please let her be staying through Christmas. I hadn't been with family on Christmas since Dad passed away. I needed, especially this year, to not be alone.

"That's the plan. Why? Do you need someone to fill your whole stocking up with those jelly candies again this year? They'll rot your pretty teeth."

"You remember that?" My dad had discovered my crush on Ike somehow, and to tease me, he'd gone the extra mile by buying several boxes of the candy of the same name and picking out the two flavors I liked most—strawberry and green apple—and filling the whole stocking to the top with them. For a couple of years, I'd lived off that supply. "My dad." I hugged a nostalgic brown velour throw pillow from beside me. "He was very good when he was good."

"Uh-huh." Aunt Gretchen didn't need to utter the opposite. Everyone, not just family, knew about Dad's illness, and the subsequent complications from it. Other people assumed, from his outward physical behaviors, that he'd had a drinking problem, but we never corrected them. Dad had insisted we let everyone think whatever they'd wanted to. "So, would you rather have the Mike & Ike's candy this year or the real thing?"

I dropped my jaw as if scandalized.

She laughed.

But that had to be nipped in the bud. "Please, *promise me* you will not do any kind of matchmaking between us. It was a hundred percent a one-sided crush. He was totally into Topanga Tycho, which means he'd never be interested in me."

Gretchen examined her nails. "That's not how I heard it."

A million particles of my soul zoomed to life, screaming for me to ask what Gretchen had heard about it, but there was a knock on the door that delivered me from that evil.

"Ladies, ladies!" Ms. Eileen came bustling into the room, all smiles and chunky plastic necklaces. She pushed her large square plastic glasses onto the top of her head. "I'm so glad you're both here." My aunt and I jumped up, and I gave Ms. Eileen a hug. "Gretchen, you'll help me persuade her, of course—since I'm letting her stay here without a contract. See? I'm a businesswoman in my own way." She squinted and smiled, and her large false teeth gleamed at us. "You have no choice, right?"

"I'm at your service, Ms. Eileen, as always." Aunt Gretchen offered Ms. Eileen the faux leather recliner and the two of us re-took the couch.

I pulled the brown velvet pillow onto my lap again, but this time to hide my inert hand. Just what, exactly, was Ms. Eileen Peters bribing Aunt Gretchen into pressuring me to do?

Both pairs of eyes fell on me.

Oh, no.

Anvils. They rained all around me. "I'm not—" I couldn't do anything for Ms. Eileen, no matter how much I loved her and owed her my whole happy youth for allowing Dad to work for her and for giving us a place to live. "I can't." My voice was nothing more than a squeak.

"You haven't even heard what Ms. Eileen is asking."

Maybe not, but the gleam in Ms. Eileen's eyes, coming right through the lenses of her plastic glasses like laser beams, told me everything. She needed someone to play the music for the Christmas Eve candle-lighting service.

Well, they'd just have to find someone else.

Chapter 2

Ike Ivey

"**B**lash!" My brush slipped, leaving a skewed smear of pastel-blue paint on the white trim between the panels on the south-facing wall. Three full weeks on this gargantuan job, and I'd avoided mess-ups completely. Then, place me under the gaze of Hazel Hollings for less than thirty seconds, and I fall into ineptitude.

Well, make that *fall even farther into ineptitude.*

"Blash!"

"No blashing in the chapel, please." Ms. Eileen stood in the doorway, her arms folded over her ample chest. "Unless it makes you feel better. Let me try it. *Blash!* Humph. You're right. It helps." She slumped down on the pew at the back of the chapel and began muttering to herself.

I'd never seen Ms. Eileen like this before. "Is something wrong?" I set my paint roller in the near-empty pan and leaned the handle against my ladder. "If it's the mistake I made with the paint, I can fix it. There's such a thing as paint thinner and rags." I should go sit down by her, listen to her. That's what a doctor with a good bedside manner would do.

I stayed near the ladder, since I'd never be that now.

"*Wrong?* It's terribly wrong. But don't you go getting wrapped up in my worries."

"If there's anything—"

She whipped to face me, her Mardi Gras green and red plastic necklaces rattling, and her giant-lensed glasses atop her head skewing to one side. "No, Isaac. I take that back. I *do* want you to get wrapped up in my worries."

If those worries involved Hazel Hollings, I was already wrapped. And tied with a bow. Just seeing that smattering of freckles again was like tossing me under the tree wearing a tag marked, "Goner." But she was even prettier now. Maybe her eyes were glistening or something, in the light from the windows, but she'd looked like an angel standing there, and I almost didn't recognize her. After all, she'd been gone from Massey Falls for four years.

Of course, there was the awful truth that way back when, I'd torched any chance I might ever have had of her liking me back—about ten times over—and my life since then had not produced any pile of evidence that I was any less of a risky option now.

Not to sound pathetic.

But there was no way at this point that Hazel Hollings would ever see me as the *young man of promise* her dad had identified me as. No house, no career, my family thought I was a loser. All my earnings went to pay the rent on that climate-controlled storage unit, and—

"How so?" I finally stopped my doom spiral. "If there's something I can do to help, let me know."

Ms. Eileen brightened, like she was a Christmas tree and someone had plugged in her lights. "Oh, bless ya, Isaac. There's nothing I'd love more than for you to paint the ceiling of the chapel. Say you'll do it. We have VIPs visiting from Reedsville for the candle lighting service on Christmas Eve, and I'd love nothing more than for the ceiling to be extra special for that night."

I came over to stand beside her, leaning against the pew across from where she sat. "Did you talk it over with Newt?" Newt might have other painting jobs lined up for me already, although they were slowing down for the holidays. I'd have to check the schedule. "I'll need to ask him if my hours can be increased, since the ceiling wasn't in his original scope of work." My neck hurt already, just thinking about the time on the ladder, leaning back. I rubbed it reflexively.

"Don't go getting a neck-ache on me, Isaac Ivey. I've ordered the scaffolding already, since I was sure you'd say yes."

Scaffolding would definitely help. "If you want, I'll order more paint from the hardware store."

"Hardware store! Is that where you buy it?"

"Where else?" It seemed like Ms. Eileen would know this basic fact of life. "I'm sure George has it on file. It might take a couple of gallons."

One hard stare, and then Ms. Eileen burst into laughter. "Oh, not that kind of painting. *Real* painting. The kind *you* do."

My whole body froze as solid as the icicles on the eaves of Falls View Chapel. "You want ... a mural?"

"I don't know what it's called! I want a painting. I want Falls View Chapel to be a tiny echo of Vatican City. This is your moment, mister. Are you going to take this opportunity, or do I have to call up Trey Tycho and tell him to cancel his plans for Christmas Eve, that there will be nothing for him to see."

Trey Tycho! An image of his blond brush mustache and his angry eyes whacked hard. My frozen limbs insta-melted, and I was a puddle on the hardwood floor. Luckily, the plastic drop cloths were down so I didn't leave a water stain. "Why would Trey Tycho come to Massey Falls for Christmas Eve? He's—he's—"

Ms. Eileen waved away my stuttering. "I know. We *all* know what Trey Tycho is. The magnate of all things art in the whole region. If it weren't for Trey Tycho, Reedsville would still be the cultural backwater with nothing but a hockey team to show for itself. We who appreciate the arts owe him our deepest gratitude for bringing the whole area to life. It's not just fine art either—though he's made our area into the new century's version of Santa Fe, I must say. You've seen what he's done with music."

Honestly, I hadn't paid as much attention to that. "All I know is he started up that museum." And ten specialized galleries. Oh, I'd give practically *anything* for my pile of framed artwork to come out of that dark storage unit and see the light of one of Tycho's galleries. "And the artists whose works he features in his galleries command quite the prices."

It was probably stupid that dollar signs danced in my head, sparkling more than sugarplums ever could. *But if I sold a painting— even one—for a Tycho-level asking price ... if my parents saw that, they might someday forgive me for disappointing them.*

"Umm-hmm." A Cheshire Cat-like smile spread over her face, showing all her teeth. "It's going to be a special night for sure, young man. But only if you're willing to fix up Falls View Chapel for us. You know, to make it worth his while."

Was Ms. Eileen acting like my patron right now? She couldn't possibly know how far I'd fallen. How completely crushed my dream was at this moment. Could she?

Then again, maybe it was written all over my face.

Finally, I snapped out of my self-absorption. "I'll do it. Do you have a theme in mind? And was there something wrong earlier?"

"No theme. And yes, so I'll need your help with that, too."

"What type of help?" Seriously, I probably looked like the town Christmas tree right now, all lit up with gratitude for Ms. Eileen giving me this insanely rare shot at getting noticed. "Anything you ask."

"I want you to get Hazel Hollings to play the organ for our candle-lighting service. I commissioned some music particularly written just for her to play that night."

Easy! Nothing easier in the history of easy. "You got it. Count on me."

Plus, that meant we might get to spend some time together in the chapel, if she was practicing organ music and I was painting.

This might work out well in several ways.

"Yes, yes." Ms. Eileen pulled herself to her feet and headed for the side doors. "It's going to be exquisite—if you can pull it off."

Why did Ms. Eileen sound so doubtful? Was there something about Hazel that I didn't know? I ran my fingers across the sleeve of the sweater she'd knitted for her dad back in the day, just as the chapel's back doors creaked open. There stood Hazel.

That white sweater made her look like an angel again, and the light from the hallway illuminated her already shining hair. It took me a second to shake off the feeling of epiphany.

"Hazel!" I jogged over to her in just a few strides. She was shorter than I remembered, but then again, I'd grown about a foot since I last saw her. "I didn't get to say hello earlier. It's me, Ike."

Was it my name that made her look green around the gills? She seemed to gulp and give a barely perceptible nod. "I remember," she said softly.

She remembered me! Something whooshed through me, cool and cleansing. "How have you been?"

"Ah," was all she said. Her gaze flew past me and fixed on the organ. It stayed there for a few seconds, until she squeezed her eyes shut for a moment. "How about you?" she asked without really looking at me. More like *through* me.

"The same *ah* as you, I guess. Until just now, that is. Ms. Eileen just offered to let me do some artwork."

Finally, Hazel returned from her reverie, her eyes actually meeting mine. "She hired you for a commission? Dad said you had been painting. *Painting* painting. That he'd encouraged you."

He'd mentioned that? "Yeah. I was for a while." No sense talking about that disastrous outcome. "He was a good friend. Good at helping people find their hidden talents."

Hazel looked back at the organ and let out a heavy breath. "Well, congratulations." She turned as if to go.

"Just a second." I caught the hem of her sweater to stop her. "Can I ask you for a favor?"

Her face hardened. "That depends." Her voice would've been ice-blue if I'd had to paint it.

"Depends on …?"

"On if you're going to ask me to play the organ on Christmas Eve."

Now, my blood ran ice-blue. I'd promised Ms. Eileen. I *owed* Ms. Eileen! What should I say? "What if I was going to ask that?"

"If you ask, I'll tell you what I told Ms. Eileen downstairs: absolutely not."

But! My hopes took one of those polar-bear plunges—until I remembered the two big gifts Ms. Eileen had mentioned. "Did you hear that Ms. Eileen commissioned organ music for the occasion?"

"I hope she can find someone to play it." Her tone chilled my bone marrow. "Otherwise, it was a waste of time and money."

That was ridiculous. This whole conversation was turning my world upside down. Hazel Hollings was unquestionably the top musician the instrument at the front of the chapel had ever met.

Something was definitely wrong. I gave her a hard look. She gave me one back, not budging. So, I played my ace card.

"Maybe you haven't heard, but there is going to be a special guest that night— the one and only Trey Tycho." Until that moment, I hadn't recalled that *the* Trey Tycho was also the one and only father of my ex-girlfriend. So many things had changed since that awful day when she kicked me to the curb. And I'd never really met him while Topanga and I were dating, he'd been so busy raising a billion dollars to bring world-class musicians to the region. Because his initial focus had been on music, and he hadn't branched into the visual arts at that time, and because back when Topanga and I were dating art wasn't on my radar, I'd never put the two together. "You've heard of him, of course."

Of course, she had. She was Hazel Hollings, the star organist for the Reedsville International Choir at the Tycho Center for the Arts on the university campus—the only building in Reedsville with as much parking available as the hockey arena. Hazel probably ate dinner at his house on a regular basis, so who was I kidding.

There's a paint color, one that Bob Ross himself loved dearly:

liquid white. I'd never actually seen it occur in real life, it was that bright. Well, other than a snowy mountainside on a sunny morning. That is, I hadn't seen it until Hazel Hollings's face went exactly that color.

"Trey Tycho?" she croaked.

And then, Hazel, wearing only her thin sweater and no coat, raced out the chapel doors and into the snow.

"Hazel! Wait!" I hollered, but she was gone.

Chapter 3

Hazel

I clutched my heart and bent over double, my breath burning my lungs.

Was this what a panic attack felt like? I'd seen them on television and in movies, but no one ever told me it was like an elephant dancing on your chest and a million baby dragons blowing fire inside your brain.

At least that's how this felt. I couldn't gulp breath fast enough.

If there had been any question before about my playing for the candle-lighting service on Christmas Eve, this sealed it. No way. Not even if Santa offered me every single present on his sleigh. I finally straightened myself and started walking down the hillside toward town. The roadway from Massey Falls proper up to the Falls View Chapel was a series of hairpin turns, alternating between steep slopes and flat areas. Believe me, that had come as a challenge in my old manual-transmission Toyota. I'd had to reach across myself to shift with my left hand. Unless things improved with my grip soon—whether or not my fingers ever worked again—I'd have to sell Dad's old car, the one thing I still had of his, since I could barely drive it, and not safely.

"Oh, you needed a walk?" Ike's paint truck putted up beside me, his window was down.

Hadn't he witnessed my total freakout? Why wasn't he mentioning it? Well, if he could ignore it, maybe I should, too.

"Want a ride?" Steam billowed as he spoke. The weather was

much colder in Massey Falls this time of year than at Reedsville's lower elevation. "I'm going down to the library. We can pick up some mystery novels, if you want to borrow them on my card. You still like mysteries?"

Forgetting everything for a second except how cold it was out there, I went around and got in on the passenger side. "You remember I liked mysteries?" His question side-tracked me and I forgot to be horrified about the whole organ-and-Tycho situation for a minute. "I read every single copy of Nancy Drew our school library had on its shelves."

"And all the Encyclopedia Brown books, too."

"Those were in elementary school!" Before I discovered the organ. "How do you even know about my Encyclopedia Brown obsession?"

"Ah, your dad talked a lot." He pushed the sweater's sleeves to his elbows. When his grip returned to the steering wheel, the muscles in his forearms flexed and pulsed.

My face heated. I averted my eyes. This was Ike. Dad and Ike were friends. Ike never had an interest in *me,* just in Dad. He'd dated the much more popular and talented and charismatic Topanga Tycho, with her piles of ash-blonde hair, curled to perfection, and her deep brown eyes and perfect makeup and fashion.

Ugh, Tychos. The banes of my existence.

"Dad loved to read. He read the Nancy Drew books to me, so I loved them too."

"That's cool." Ike steered us through the snow-covered pines toward town. "Discovered any good authors lately?"

I named a few. Some he'd heard of, others not. We talked about books, and Ms. Eileen, and nothing the rest of the way to the library. Somehow, Ike must have sensed that I needed a break from the topic of music and art and Trey Tycho. Bless him for it.

Inside the library, he headed off to look for his books while I gazed at the fish tank, listened to the toddler-storytime lady read *How the Grinch Stole Christmas* and *The Three Trees* to the little children, and marveled at all the crèche displays made by the after-school-program kids. By the time Ike had completed his checkout, I could breathe normally again, and the ache was gone from my chest.

How had he achieved that for me? My eyes strayed to his forearms again, as they held the pile of books to his chest.

"I got you something." He held up a familiar book. "It's the vintage cover. Massey Falls never updated this series."

He placed the well-worn book into my left hand, his fingers brushing the skin of my palm. Tingles skittered. I squeezed my fingers shut around the book's spine and held the cover up close to my face so he couldn't see the redness of my cheeks.

"Is everything all right? Are you cold?" Ike stopped walking. "I'm pretty sure they sell hoodies in the bookstore. I can get you one."

"Thanks. I'm all right." *Sort of.* What I really was, was a twitterpated schoolgirl with a crush on a book character who looked like my real-life childhood crush. Yep, as a kid, Ike Ivey had borne a pretty strong resemblance to the vintage illustrations of Encyclopedia Brown: lanky, intelligent-looking, clear-eyed, interested in everything, that shock of straight hair always bothering his forehead.

And Ike's face on the front and in the illustrations inside are why I read them! They're why I read them all!

Gah! How meta was this moment right now? If my face got any hotter, it would burst into flames like dry pine needles subjected to old-timey Christmas lights.

"It's no problem, I swear." He shoved the rest of his books into my arms. "I'll be right back."

For the second time in an hour, I might've expired from an overload of emotion. I fought to keep my breath steady. *It's fine. Everything's fine. Ike Ivey just went to buy me a sweatshirt because he thinks I'm cold when, really, I'm having a crush-memory-attack.*

Was that even a thing? If it hadn't been one before, I was now living proof.

"I hope you don't mind, this was the only one they had in your size." The decal featured the Grinch holding up a leg of roast beast and grinning. It was weird. Festive, but weird.

Ike took the books from me, and I pulled the sweatshirt over my head, careful not to expose my hand to his view. Then, once it was on me, it took all my self-control not to pop the attached hood up and shrink down inside it like Yertle the Turtle.

"Thank you," I said, and we headed back out to his work truck. "And I'm sorry about earlier. I'm not really myself lately."

"About that …"

Oh, no. He was going to ask. Should I tell him? Even Aunt Gretchen didn't know yet. No, I couldn't. It was too raw, and, based on recent events, I'd probably crumble.

Ike held open the passenger side door, and I climbed in. He placed the stack of books on my lap. "Is this okay?"

"Sure." I glanced down at his choices of reading material. They were all art books, large and small, with religious motifs—everything from medieval art of the Holy Family to contemporary block-and-line minimalism that was hyper-symbolic. "What are you studying these for?"

He was already in the driver's seat and started the truck. It snorted to life. The back seat was filled with rattling paint supplies, and the steering wheel was covered with little splotches of latex paint. The work truck belonged to Mr. Newt, the owner of the painting service. Maybe Ike wasn't supposed to be taking side trips to the library. Mr. Newt was kind of strict, if I remembered him well.

"Oh, those?" Ike darted a glance over at the pile. "It's, um." He slowed down for the stoplight near Victorian Revival, the home renovation company my friend Bryony worked for. "Well, you know how Ms. Eileen can be."

"Did she try to rope you into something too?"

"Not *try* to rope me in. Did rope me in."

I got it. "When it comes to Ms. Eileen, there is only do. There is no try." My Yoda voice lacked.

"The force is strong with that one." He shot me a grimace.

Well, she wasn't going to force *me* into anything—not because I didn't love and appreciate her, but frankly, because it wasn't even possible for me to do what she asked. We hit a pothole and my faulty hand stung as if to prove my point.

"So, what's your Ms. Eileen task?" It was better to direct the conversation toward him, and away from me. "Are you going to sing in the choir?"

Of *course,* my first instinct was toward music. Gah! Why did my brain fog up so much when I was around Ike? For the past three months, I think I'd mentioned music fewer than three times aloud. Now, *this.*

"She wants me to paint the ceiling."

"Holy neck-ache." I tucked the book he gave me into my purse to savor later.

"Right? But she got scaffolding for me."

"Really?" Scaffolding would be a pain to set up, considering it was probably only a two-day job at most. "That was thoughtful. What color will it be? Sky blue, like the walls?"

Ike stabbed a finger at the book atop the stack on my lap. "I haven't decided what to paint yet."

In a flash, Ms. Eileen's task for Ike dawned on me. "You're *painting* painting the ceiling? As in Falls View Chapel is the local version of the Sistine Chapel, and as in, you'll be the Michelangelo di Lodovico Buonaroti of Massey Falls?"

"Girl knows her Italian Renaissance artists. Full names and all."

"I went through a fierce Florence, Italy, phase. Plus, I had a full semester of High Renaissance music. So many masses, motets, and madrigals. For one of my recitals, there was a choir who followed along doing chansons."

"That vocabulary is so lost on me. I'm self-taught. And my version of fine art is …" He got very quiet.

"Is what?"

"Is not really the *thing* for a church ceiling."

"You paint naked ladies? Because Michelangelo did his share of nudes, you know." Ike's face turned deep red. Had I just used the words *naked* and *nude* in a single sentence while talking to Ike Ivey? *About church?* My awkwardness knew no limits today. How could I even recover? Quickly, I blathered on with, "Just kidding. What is your art style?"

He winced while still looking at the road. "Western."

Immediately, I pictured men wearing cowboy hats, holding lassos, riding muscular horses through streams in desert scenes. "Western," I parroted. "And she asked you to paint that on the ceiling?"

"She didn't give me any direction. She said I'd know what to do."

Ohhh. That was possibly even worse. "That makes me think of times when I need to bring something to a potluck dinner. How can I possibly know what to bring? It's too much pressure."

"Good analogy. But I always want to bring the same thing to a potluck: *krumkake*. Of course, I never do, but if I did, that's what I'd bring."

"Your grandma used to make those." The road back to the chapel curved and rose. "I remember. They're the cone-shaped waffle cookies, right? With the pattern on them?" Crisp, sweet, with their own unique spice—they were Scandinavia's best export, if you asked me.

"She was famous for them. I make them now and then and eat the whole batch."

That sounded suspiciously lonely. Wasn't Ike still dating Topanga? Everyone had told me through the grapevine a few years before that their marriage was a lock. Maybe a long engagement happened. It was hard to believe that Topanga would let Ike Ivey slip through her fingers.

We arrived in the chapel's parking lot. Ike shut off the engine, but he didn't get out. He just looked at me. "I don't know if I can do it."

My response came quick as lightning, no missed breath. "You can, Ike."

He locked eyes with me, and it felt like little pebbles of E=mc^2

19

flowed between us, creating energy and light in an exciting series of bangs each time one collided with my corneas. If I moved, I could be the source of nuclear fission and explode the whole hillside on which sat the Falls View Chapel.

"I'm not sure, Hazel. It's been so long."

"You can. I'll help you."

He jutted his chin forward. "You mean it?"

"Absolutely. I mean, don't give me a brush to use, but I'll cheer you on from afar."

"I need help from a-near."

The thought of being near him sizzled through me. *Ike Ivey just asked me to be near him.* I shook it off as fast as I could. "How near? I'm afraid of heights. The scaffolding might freak me out."

"Me, too. But you don't have to climb the scaffold. It's better if only one person is on that, in case of, I don't know, bumping into each other." He patted his elbows.

My eyes darted to his forearms involuntarily. I pried them away again to look at his face. "Yeah, no bumping into each other." Much as my body chemistry was saying otherwise, I agreed. "I want to help, not hinder. What do you suggest?"

A moment passed. He rubbed his chin. There was a faint stubble that hadn't been there earlier, when I first saw him in the chapel. It made him seem so masculine. That, and the forearms. Was I a total crush-drunk mess? Possibly. "You might not like it."

"Try me." *Please say that kissing will inspire you.*

He did not say kissing. He said the worst thing I could have imagined.

"Music helps me focus. Mood tunes, you know? Any chance you'd play some Christmas songs on the organ while I work?"

Chapter 4

Ike

When Hazel had charged out of the chapel earlier in the day, I thought I'd never seen her move so fast. Well, that was just a foreshadowing of speed to come, because the second I mentioned the possibility of her providing the background music, the mood tunes, for my painting project, she shot out of Mr. Newt's Paint-mobile faster than all of the other reindeer turning their backs when Rudolph asked if he could play with them.

"I'm really sorry, Ms. Eileen." I shrugged as I gave her the stack of books. She sat at the desk in the church's office, which already had two decorated trees—one full-sized and another tiny on her desk that spun and played "Silent Night" with music-box tinkling. "I doubt your plan will work. The mere mention of it shifted her speed to white lightning. She made it patently obvious she's not going to play for the candle-lighting service."

Ms. Eileen dropped her face onto clenched fists. Her super-sized eyeglasses fell off the top of her head and clattered onto the desk. "But the music is absolutely *made* for her. Literally." She looked up. "I commissioned Jesse Parrish with the express instructions that he tailor it to her musical abilities and preferred style. He spent a full week analyzing Hazel's performances at the Tycho Center, and then additional weeks creating this piece specifically for her. It's one of a kind, and she is the ideal person to play it." She went on about aspects of the composition that I couldn't hope to comprehend. "Please, Ike.

You've got to convince her, or else it's all for nothing, all Jesse's work."

Jesse Parrish. "Wait a minute. He's the man who won the award for that movie score. *That* Jesse Parrish? How did you get him?"

"Believe me, it wasn't easy. His schedule is insane, but he loves Christmas, and especially organ music at Christmas played well. Which is why it's such a tragedy if Hazel keeps resisting. What is going on with her, do you think?"

I had no idea. But until I found out, it was clear Ms. Eileen's specially commissioned composition was going to get no air-time during the candle-lighting service this year. "Did you request it because you knew Trey Tycho was coming to our event?"

"How did you know?"

"I'm good with hunches."

"I bet you are. Well, Isaac, my dear. Get yourself a hunch about that stubborn girl—the one who never used to be stubborn a day in her life, other than toward herself and being rigorous about putting in the time needed to perfect her skills at playing the pipe organ. It's too sad if she lets that part of herself go."

That hit the nail on the head. Hazel couldn't let whatever was bothering her stop her from being who she was. Music was too big a part of her to give up. No matter what was going on.

"I'll try my best. But my hunch is telling me I've got my work cut out for me." I pointed to the stack of books. "Can you reconsider, though? Would you at least look through these art history compilations and see whether something inspires you? I—I can't let you down." Or Trey Tycho. Or the congregants of the Falls View Chapel. They deserved a beautiful ceiling, and I didn't want to mess it up.

But Ms. Eileen just pushed the stack back toward me. "It's not about what inspires *me*, it's what inspires you. And I chose *you* for a reason, Isaac. You must realize that there are at least a dozen talented artists here in town, but you are the person I selected. Think about it."

That was the problem—I couldn't stop thinking about it. All last night, I'd tossed and turned in my bed, thinking about the ceiling and how it could go *so wrong*. Worse, about the short timeline. There was less than a month until Christmas Eve. What artist could paint such a large space—with any level of professional skill—in that scant amount of time? Okay, thoughts of Hazel Hollings's curves as the sweatshirt slipped over her head also kept my eyes propped open as if with toothpicks. As she'd raised her arms, her top had lifted to reveal the tiniest sliver of her milky white skin at her jeans' waistband.

It made me feel like some kind of creeper for recalling it, but anytime I was near her, she kept me in knots. Or in piles of unknotted ropes, just chaotic and useless. Spaghetti in a gnarly wad on the plate.

Too many metaphors, not enough sense in them.

"All right," I said at last and gathered the books. I slunk out of her office.

"Oh, Ike?" Ms. Eileen called after me, and I turned back to listen. *She never refers to me as Ike.* "You're going to create something exquisite. I can feel it in my bones."

"Thanks." I forced a smile. "Your confidence in me won't go to waste."

I hoped.

An hour later, I sat on a side pew at the back of the chapel with my artist's sketchpad, a dozen pages of brainstorms deep, with no solid plan. Nothing felt right. The center shaft of the pencil I held had been chewed into near oblivion, and I could possibly get lead-poisoning from the amount of yellow paint on its exterior that I'd ingested. *Think! Think! Be inspired!* I turned the page, dragged my pencil across the space, picturing the expanse of the ceiling, shaping it in my mind, adjusting for the curvature of the wall—for it did have a concavity that could make it much more beautiful *if* I could use that to my advantage.

To my surprise, the pencil seemed to come to life this time, creating images almost of its own volition—from somewhere deep in my subconscious. Plants, animals, skyscape, action, drama, hope. It all blossomed on the page before my eyes and beneath the gliding point of the pencil.

Wow, look at *that*. I marveled at my creation. It wasn't exactly church ceiling material, but it was easily the best thing I'd drawn for pre-painting in ages. Maybe ever. The lines flowed, the power exuded, the message was both symbolic and clear at once.

I love it.

I hadn't loved anything I'd created in a long time. Well, I hadn't created anything unique in a very long time. Months, maybe longer. I sat back and stared at it in wonder. Why here? Why now? I looked up and around the empty room, and …

It wasn't until that moment when I realized—the whole empty hall was actually full. Not with people, but with sound, soft and sweet and mellow. Because it had just been low, swelling tones of bass notes, and a barely placeable melody, I hadn't even noticed when it began.

But there, at the east end of the chapel, ensconced in the spot I'd seen her occupy a thousand days of my life long ago, sat Hazel.

And she was playing the organ.

And changing me from afraid to confident, from blocked to flowing, from mouse to man.

Hazel—my mind stretched out to speak to her silently, as if we already had some kind of connection, which was all in my imagination, of course—*thank you.*

Now, why did that song sound so familiar? It was an unusual one and not a very religious choice of song for inside a chapel, but which fit Massey Falls to a tee—it was like a frothy mix of the *chestnuts roasting* song everyone knew and the *weather is frightful but let it snow so we can kiss* song. I might have sighed, because she looked up.

"Oh!" She hit a sour chord. "I didn't know anyone was here." She slipped off the bench, put on her shoes, and headed for the side door. "Sorry." She pressed it open, and she was gone before the gratitude could even reach my lips.

Blash! Blash it again!

Chapter 5

Hazel

If I'd known Ike was in the chapel, I never would've ventured to turn on the organ, let alone sit my sorry self down on the bench, change into my organ slippers which were still inside the bench, adjust the stops, or—even worse—attempt to play. I wouldn't have softly tested out the lower register with my only working hand, or pressed on the bass pedals below the keyboard, even with the volume at its absolute lowest.

No, if I'd seen him curled up on that back pew, I would have darted away even faster than I had from his truck, like the down of a thistle, as the poem went.

Instead, I now ran through the church's hallway and into one of the classrooms—the one with the working radiator. I huddled up next to it on the floor, and inhaled the familiar scent of chalk dust and sweaty little Sunday school kids.

Why! Why, oh why, did Ike have to be there when I was at my most vulnerable? My most heartbreakingly obviously inept. I didn't want anyone to know how low I'd fallen—least of all Ike.

The shocked way he'd looked at me when our eyes met caught me off guard. He seemed genuinely happy and excited.

Why?

Oh, there was no one more beautiful when smiling than Ike Ivey. Not in a magazine cover way, but in one of those *glowing from the inside out* divine ways—with that magnetism which had always made him utterly irresistible to me. Oh, I needed to forget him! Why, when he'd started to date that charismatic bombshell Topanga back in high school, hadn't I forgotten him instantly? Instead, I'd learned more and more complex pieces on the organ—frightening and angry pieces like Bach's "Toccata and Fugue in D Minor" that all the creepy villains in movies play on the organ. But at least I'd had music to attempt to get him out of my system back then.

Now what could I do?

A faint knock came on the door and it creaked open. "Hazel?"

My heart lurched inside my chest, pounding against my rib bones. "Um, hi?" I swiped beneath my eyes. Whew, no tears—for once. Sure, I had the gift and curse of being an easy crier. But it came with a cheerful cousin: the gift of also being an easy laugher. Not that I felt like laughing right now. And I hadn't for a while, to be honest.

"Can I tell you something?" Ike walked right in and sat down on the floor beside where I was basically hugging the radiator. "Wow, it's warm in here. Nice. The chapel is basically an icebox."

Bless him for not asking me if I was okay. I was so over people asking whether I was okay, and he seemed to intuit that fact. Another reason I couldn't help still liking the guy. Emotional intelligence was possibly a rarer commodity than, oh, plutonium. Whatever, I was being weird.

"You have something to show me?" I said, sitting up straighter. He was holding a sketch pad. Ah, that made sense. "You were drawing." Probably in preparation for his ceiling art. "I didn't know you were in the chapel. Sorry if I interrupted your work."

"Funny, I hadn't realized you were in there either."

But—but, I was playing the organ. How could he not—? Never mind. Again, bless the guy! "Did you complete a sketch?"

"Yes, but it's not quite what any other chapel ceiling should be." He pressed the open page to his chest.

"Are you ready to show anyone?" A million little particles inside me wished he would say yes and that he'd chosen *me* to be the recipient of the first view of it. "If not, I understand."

"No, I'd love to show you. Just—keep in mind—it's probably not what anyone is expecting." He slowly pulled the sketch book from its clutched spot at his chest. "Even Ms. Eileen, who seriously would *not* listen when I asked what she was going for."

Finally, he tilted the page toward me, and then he placed it in my left hand. I angled it into the light coming through the arched window, and then used my right elbow to press aside the curtain and allow a larger beam of sunlight to come in and illuminate the drawing.

"Wow," I breathed. "It's ..." There was no word for how it made me feel.

The strength of the horse, the valor in the eyes of the cowboy, the little sheep caught in the stream near the hooves of the steed. Looking at it, you just *knew* the cowboy would rescue the lamb from the stream's rapids.

The symbolism hit me all at once, the parable of the lost sheep.

My head voice hollered, *I'm the lost sheep. And there's some kind cowboy who will yank me from the stream before I drown.*

Okay, that's when the tears started. I was ridiculous, but I swiped at them, and they just kept coming.

"You're crying?" Ike looked stricken. "Help a guy out."

"It's a good thing, I promise." I swept them aside, and pasted on my brightest smile. "I wasn't expecting that."

He let out a huge whoosh of breath. "You're sure it's good?"

"I'm sure." As sure of that fact as of anything I'd experienced all year. "It's special, Ike."

"It never would've happened unless ..."

There was a long pause, during which he alternately looked at his shoes and out the window. He still didn't finish his sentence. Finally, I prompted him. "Unless?"

"You won't like it. I don't want to say."

My voice lowered to a whisper. "You can tell me anything, Ike."

He frowned and met my eyes. "Unless you'd been playing the

organ."

Ugh! Why did that have to be the thing he'd said? "It's not—I'm not—I can't—" But my own declaration came back to haunt me. Or, rather, humble me. "Sorry, I did say you could tell me anything." My reactions—I needed to get better control of them and quit running away anytime someone brought up playing the organ. Because here I was in Massey Falls, and everyone knew me as the girl who played the organ. It was basically my only identity, so it was inevitably going to come up. I needed to quit being so skittish and weird. Pronto.

I steadied my breath and my inner freak-out. "But you said you didn't even know I was in the chapel." I gave him back the sketch book, even though I wanted to keep the picture and place it in my room. Or in my heart. Or paint it on the insides of my eyelids so I could look at it anytime.

Slowly, he shook his head. "That's just it. I'd been in there since early this morning, hoping to catch a bit of inspiration from a muse. Page after page, I'd been sitting there drawing—badly. I could show you, but you'd recoil in horror."

"I doubt that."

"For reals." He tapped the book, and then he did that thing where you fan through several pages at once with your thumb. "They're *not* good."

I reserved judgment on that. We were sitting close beside each other on the wood floor. Part of me wanted to inch toward him, but I resisted. He might've been engaged to Topanga, for all I knew.

"Anyway, I'd sat there a while, and suddenly, the pencil seemed to flow of its own accord, and the next thing I knew, I had this." He held it up for me to see again. "It shocked me a little."

Speaking of shocks. All that electricity between us had come back. *Probably because I quit being a weirdo.* The air in that radiator room practically crackled.

"It was then that I realized you were playing the organ. You'd been playing low notes, really quietly. I looked up at you, and you stopped, excused yourself, and left."

"Sorry about that." How many times was I going to apologize? Probably a million, because I was me. At least until I shared the real reason for my crazy reaction, I'd be apologizing all over the place. If he knew, he might understand.

And pity me.

Ugh, I did not want pity.

"Your sketch is just right, Ike. You have to put that on the ceiling. I'm glad my messing around with music helped you get the inspiration you needed. That's just lucky."

"It didn't feel lucky. It felt necessary."

How nice of him to say. "Well, good luck transferring that onto the ceiling. I bet you'll make it really lifelike. And effective."

"Hazel, would you …" He looked at his feet again and then back at me, searching my face for several moments. "You're so pretty."

"What?" My stomach flipped over. I pressed a fist against it to stop the gymnastics, though. The guy had dated Topanga, for heaven's sake. "Thank you. You were saying, *would you.* Would I what?" But I knew what he was going to ask. "You need me to play the organ while you paint, don't you."

He pressed his palm to his forehead and pulled a begging smile. "I really do. There's just no time between now and Christmas Eve to create something so large. My concentration and flow are insanely higher if I have music going."

"I can create you the most excellent playlist. You can listen on ear-buds. You can—" But I knew it was no use. He needed live music. He needed the resonance filling the room from ceiling to floor.

"I need *you.*" His words caught me off guard, and it must have showed because he back-pedaled. "I mean, I need the live music, the notes you choose, the Falls View Chapel organ itself. It has its own tone, you know."

Oh, I knew. And I knew exactly what he'd meant—even though my hopeless crush wished desperately that he'd meant he needed me, personally, in all the ways. "I get it."

"You'll do it then?" He stood up and looped the room with his long legs, nervousness and excitement roiling off him like a storm. "It's a *lot* to ask. I'll have to be painting a lot of hours a day."

I was used to long hours at the organ. "If it's for the sake of the chapel. And Ms. Eileen." *And you.*

"Thank you!" He took two strides, pulled me to my feet, and caught me up in his arms. "You're the best! This could mean everything for my future career, and I can't thank you enough." He lifted me and swung me in a circle.

The exuberance was contagious.

Yes, I'd do that for him. I'd play left-hand pieces and pedals. I'd let the air in the room resonate with swells and soft notes—but I would not play on Christmas Eve during the candle-lighting service. Not if Trey Tycho was coming.

"But you can't, can *not*, tell Ms. Eileen about it. She'll rope me into doing the Christmas Eve thing, and I totally can't." Literally. The music for all the hymns for the night required two hands. I only had one.

"That might be a problem. She's basically at the chapel day and night." He opened the door, and there went Eileen, bustling past with more energy than usual even.

A shriek gurgled in my constricted throat. What had she heard?

She paused and whirled around. "Oh, there you two are! I just got off the phone after arriving late today, and now I'm a full-on mess."

That was one state of mind I could empathize with.

She fanned herself. "It's hot in there," she said, indicating the radiator room. "I need to get the repairman in here to fix that. Anyway, I'm glad you're together so I only have to say this once. My daughter, Sheila—you remember her, right?—went into early labor over in Mendon, and she needs me to come right now to take care of her three older children. I have no idea how long I'll be gone. Days or weeks, but definitely not on the night of the candle-lighting service. She's due before that, thank the heavens above. Meanwhile, you two can handle things at the church, right? I already talked to Gretchen about managing the phones, and she said she'd get them forwarded to her cell, and—Oh, I'm sorry, but I just have to get on the road. Poor Sheila!" She headed for the door.

"Ms. Eileen?" Ike strode after her, extending the sketch book. "Do you want to approve my idea for the ceiling art?"

She waved it off and just walked faster—a speed-waddle. "I trust you."

"Should you, though?"

The guy sold himself short. The idea was gold. I wanted to shout it at both of them, but it wasn't time, and I'd been left many paces behind them.

Either way, that settled that.

Ms. Eileen would be gone, so Ike and I could spend every day together in the chapel without my needing to freak out and worry about being discovered. There would be a blessed reprieve from the Christmas Eve pressure and, hopefully, from Aunt Gretchen's notorious matchmaking pressure, too.

The only thing left was to keep myself from falling for Ike all over again. Because I could not take another heartbreak this calendar year. Or maybe in my whole life. I'd better put up all my heart-guards, or I was doomed.

Chapter 6

Ike

The scaffolding was up the next morning. Somehow, Ms. Eileen had orchestrated that from her babysitting perch over in Mendon. That, or she'd scheduled it before leaving town.

Which left me lying on my back staring at the ceiling a couple of feet above me—paralyzed. How could I even begin? The sun was already up and streaming through the curtains of the chapel, but my arm would not lift the first brush to fill even in the area I'd set aside for sky and clouds.

"You're not painting." Hazel's voice pierced the silence, startling me. How long had she been in the room?

"You're not playing." I didn't mean to accuse her, but it might have come across that way.

"I'm blocked." She said it so matter-of-factly. It was a much better reaction than I'd expected, after all the startle-reflex moments over the past few days. Maybe she was going to be okay. I wished she'd tell me what was wrong.

"Me, too." I dragged out a sigh. "What if I mess up?"

"Then, you'll just paint over it. There are lots of chances."

Yeah, if I had an infinite amount of time between now and when it needed to be complete. "Maybe I'll start at the edges."

"What are you going to put there?"

"Not sure yet." I sat up on my elbow and looked over the edge of the scaffolding at her. Her dusting of freckles and her generous smile caught me, like a soul hiccup. "What are you going to play today?"

"Not sure yet."

We were both stuck. The truth was, I'd been stuck for months. Ever since the big gallery in Los Angeles sent me the curt rejection letter. *We don't show Western art unless it's by an artist who commands six figures.* Of course not, since they were in it for the money. It made good business sense.

I hadn't sold anything at all. Even a small painting. I had my reasons for that, but they looked a little small-minded if I wasn't careful to stick to my standards. *No sales unless they're for what the painting is truly worth.* I'd rather hoard them than undercut myself.

Which was why I was stuck working for Mr. Newt, paying top dollar to store the canvases out of the elements. Mom and Dad wouldn't hear any pleas to allow me to store them in their spare room. I'd breathed the possibility and been blasted all to smithereens two Christmases ago.

Never again.

"If you start, I will." Her voice floated up to me.

"I didn't think that was what we agreed would work."

"Neither did I, but remember—yesterday, you were drawing first. I wasn't playing first."

The logic escaped me, but I mixed some cerulean blue on the palette with a touch of cobalt blue until it felt right, and then I applied it to the middle of the ceiling, about a third of the way through the panel. The curve was easier to work with than I'd expected, and the paint spread easily on the plaster. I used another brush to apply a slightly lighter shade. Eventually, it faded into yet another shade of the same tone, in an ombre fashion all the way to the side of the panel.

Yes. That was working. Over time, I carefully applied the technique to more and more of the area. The sky across about ten percent of the panel had sprung into being. It was taking shape, and suddenly—I *knew*. I knew what came next.

I set down the blue brush and picked up my tube of french ultramarine, squeezing a dot of it onto my board, and then added some titanium white to make it as bright as possible. In one swift action, I applied it—*a star*. Then, I took up my fan brush and feathered the area all around the star, brighter near its core and dimming as it spread, adding a few beams of starlight here and there.

Exhale. I shook out my hand and fingers and wrist. There! That wasn't so hard. And Hazel hadn't even started to …

Wait a second. The music *did,* in fact, fill the room. Just like yesterday, she'd chosen the lower notes and the pedal tones, very low.

"Hazel?" I leaned over the edge of the scaffolding. She lifted her left hand from the keyboard and then tucked it beneath her thigh. "What time is it?"

"Nearly four. I'm starving. I thought you'd never come out of that creation coma."

Ha. That was a great term for it. "You were playing all this time?"

Her head tilted to one side. "You really didn't know?"

"Oh, some part of me knew. That's why I was able to complete so much of the sky. Can you see it from there?" I moved out of the way, and aimed a thumb toward the work.

"You added a star. I like it. Is it the morning or the evening star?"

"Evening." Despite the fact I hadn't given that any thought before then, I knew instinctively I'd done the evening star. "I'll add a sunrise over there." I pointed to the opposite end of the panel.

"Our daystar rising. I get it. I once played a piece with that title."

I didn't get it, but she was the one who knew music, not me. "Daystar. The sun. Now, I get it." Then, I caught hold on what she'd said a minute ago. "Can I take you to get something to eat?"

Her arms folded in on themselves, and she tucked her hands into her armpits. "Um, I'm not sure."

"Come on. I'll treat you. Any place you want to go. Do you want a sit-down meal? I could go for a steak at El Toro." Not that I had money for steak most of the time, but Mr. Newt had paid me that morning and

34

my account had a little bit of spare change. "They make a great steak, *huevos rancheros*-style. Have you tried it?"

"Yes, but no steak. Please." She almost shuddered. Was she a vegetarian these days? "I could go for a burger and fries, though." Her form relaxed. "If you'll promise me one thing—that you'll bring me all the little paper cups of ketchup from the pump that I ask for."

"You got it." A small price to pay. "Let's go."

A half hour later, I met her in the red vinyl booth, carrying the plastic tray with our burgers, fries, and fresh strawberry shakes.

"We could freeze, eating ice cream in this weather." She bit the paper sleeve off her straw and stuck the straw into the top of her cup.

"I'm willing to risk it. Plus, they offer hot chocolate, so we could get that afterward to counteract the cold. Warning, though, their hot chocolate is so hot when you get it that you have to either add ice or else take the lid off and blow on it for a while so you don't cook yourself from the inside out when you drink it."

"Noted." She took a long sip of her shake. "Maybe we could just sit and chat while we wait for it to cool." She stiffened. "I mean, if you want to sit and chat with me. If you don't have other places to be. People you're obligated to."

Hardly. "I have time to chat." With Hazel, I could probably talk for hours, for whatever reason—maybe because of what her dad had done for me back in the day. His sweater's sleeves had slipped, so I pushed them back up to my elbows.

Hazel glanced down at my arms. She stared for a minute. Then, she looked up, and acted like she'd been caught doing something wrong.

Wait a second. Had she *noticed* me? Like, in that way?

Not possible. She was Hazel Hollings, and I was … no one. Less than no one, now that I'd made all my *loser choices.* My parents could've trademarked the term *loser choices.* No way would someone as incredibly talented and successful as Hazel give me a passing glance.

Although, she'd given much more than a passing glance at my arm a second ago.

I checked for paint smears.

"You have my dad's sweater."

Oh, so that was it. Did I deflate? A little. "I wondered when you'd notice."

"I noticed the first second I saw you wearing it."

That made sense. "He said you crocheted it."

"Knitted."

"There's a difference?"

She kicked my ankle under the table. Just a little, but I felt it on several levels. "Ike! They're totally different." She went into the details, like the fact crochet has one hook, and knitting has two needles—sans hooks. There were a lot more facts involved, but I got a little in the weeds about it because I kept staring at her freckles, and at the way her eyes sparkled, and the full pout of her lips.

She really did have the prettiest face I'd ever seen.

Dorky me, I'd told her so yesterday in the radiator room. Luckily, she'd given it the attention it deserved—none, if it came from me, king of the loser choices.

"So, by mistaking knit for crochet, are you saying I disqualified myself from asking for a knitted sweater of my own?" There I went again! Flirting like I was worthy of her. "Just kidding, just kidding."

The spark in her snuffed out. "It's nothing to do with you."

We ate in silence for a minute. Blash! She was hiding something, I could tell. All her life, she'd been the openest of open books. Now, she kept snapping shut at the merest word. I had to figure this out at some point—if only so I could quit, I don't know, trampling her heart.

I left and brought her two more little paper cups of ketchup. "Dunk away." I started whistling a little tune from the back of my brain—the one that was always my default setting.

Her french fry paused in midair, halfway to her mouth. She was listening. I let the whistling peter out.

"No, keep going."

36

"What?"

"That song. Keep going with it."

Um, okay? I gave it a few more notes, and her eyes flew open.

"How do you know that song?"

"It's the music at the back of my brain. How do you know it? Are you going on strolls through my mind?" *Ha, ha. Very funny. The girl practically has an all-day, every day, walking route mapped out in my mind, even though she doesn't know it.* "I heard it a long time ago. It's really catchy."

"You think so?" She set down her french fry and gave a quick shudder. "This is the craziest moment." She opened a packet of salt and poured it on nothing. "I—I wrote that song, though it's not finished."

"Seriously?" Now, I set down my fries, all four that were gathered in one big wad. "Then how do I know it?"

"That's the question. Did my dad sing it to you?"

"There are words?" If so, I didn't know them. "Sorry, it's just something—wait a second. Yes, your dad did pass it along to me. But he didn't sing it, he whistled it. We would rake leaves or trim the juniper trees or trim the lilacs, and he'd whistle. One time, he told me to join in, so I did, and so we whistled it all season. Among other songs. He was a champion whistler."

Her features softened, and her gaze took on a faraway look. "Really, he was." She smiled. "I'd totally forgotten about that song until yesterday. It's called 'Christmas With You.'"

Good to know. I'd never really pondered whether it had a title. "Are there words, then?"

The burger place suddenly got very loud, as a group of high school students barged in, yelling and bouncing a basketball and laughing. So much for conversation over hot cocoa. We packed up our tray, and I threw out the trash.

Back in the truck, we made our way through town. Every inch of Massey Falls exuded the festive notes of Christmas. Wreaths on every lamp post, strings of lights stretching across the road between buildings, holiday music piping through the air—and, of course, the piles of snow.

As we climbed the hill back toward Falls View Chapel, I wanted to bring up the question again, but she turned toward me.

"Do you think it would distract you if I try to flesh out that song on the organ? Develop the melody there?"

"It's already the background music of my mind. It won't distract me." Especially if it was that same tune, so mellow, she'd played earlier.

"So you're saying I've invaded your brain." She waved her fingertips at me ominously, and then broke into that generous grin—the old familiar one I'd known so well when she was younger—and into that rumbling contralto laugh that did something funny to my insides.

Ah, that smile. I hadn't seen it during the whole time she'd been back in Massey Falls—until now. It warmed me more than hot cocoa. "I like your laugh."

She offered it again, like bubbles from a waterfall or a fizzy drink. "It's not something I have much control over." Then, she reached over and clapped my shoulder.

Okay, *that* action warmed me more than the boiling cocoa. The heat spread through me, not just from her touch, but from her happiness. Seeing Hazel happy was the prettiest sight of the season, and hearing her laughter was better than turkey dinner.

"Then, I'll play. Or at least try."

I glanced over, and her eyes were brimming and glistening. The prospect of writing music must be much more emotional for her than I would have guessed. It all had to harken back to whatever she was keeping from me.

And I still hadn't told her why I wore her dad's sweater every single day.

The prospect of these long days with Hazel, the two of us creating beautiful things together, or at least in tandem and close proximity, made the holiday season ahead look a lot brighter than any had in several years.

Especially if she kept glancing at my arms and touching my shoulders. And letting me swing her in a circle while I hugged her.

"Do you want to wait until tomorrow?"

"Ike! I just realized I need staff paper. Can we swing by the music store? And I don't think I can wait. You don't have to keep painting if you're worn out, but I—I think I need to start my project right away. This very evening."

Chapter 7

Hazel

My whole head was stuffed with cotton. Too many hours at the organ bench yesterday—after too many months. My muscles and brain had atrophied. But I'd come up with quite a few more bars of the Christmas song I'd doodled for Dad so long ago.

I'd had to scribble the notes onto the staff lines with my left hand. They were a mess. I'd clean them up later using a computer program before printing it out officially. As it was, I could see most of what I'd written—mostly.

"You're awake?" Aunt Gretchen walked into my bedroom, bringing me a piece of toast with butter and jam. "It's after seven. You're usually up hours ahead of me."

"Why are you up?" I sat up and took the toast off the plate. I bobbled it—my left hand would never be as adept as my right. I'd probably lost a few pounds since eating was so wonky. But toast was possible. So were burgers and fries.

Not steak. Nothing requiring a knife and fork, at least not in public. Too uncomfortable for anyone watching, for sure. And I still hadn't explained my injury to Ike. Or Gretchen. Or anyone. Not even to Trey Tycho after he'd so viciously attacked me in public—right during that performance in the autumn. Maybe that had traumatized me so much I couldn't put any of it into words.

Really, I should go see someone about it. But the thought of telling even a professional sent me spiraling.

"Me?" She answered my question from the kitchen. "I'm up because I'm still dealing with jet lag from my last trip to the Philippines." Aunt Gretchen returned holding a piece of toast of her own, this one smeared with peanut butter. "Mmm. Whole wheat bread from Yuletide Bakery is pure ambrosia. I've been everywhere, but nothing compares to the pure bliss of this bread."

"Amen." I took a bite, and only a few crumbs landed on my shirt. I used my right hand to brush them off, hoping Aunt Gretchen didn't spot the curled-up piece of cauliflower that my fist resembled. "Any plans for today?"

"They're doing a preview of the snow sculpture festival this morning. Do you want to go?"

Oh! I loved that event. It'd been a long time since I'd gone. There were so many talented people in town, and they planned their displays all year long.

"That would be really great, except I'm, um, probably spending time with, um, Ike Ivey." Good grief! Why did I have to spill that stockingful of Ike candies? "He's doing some painting and I said I'd help." There, that was vague enough, right? Made me sound altruistic. Of course it did.

"Ike Ivey. He's a good one, so you know I approve." Aunt Gretchen chewed another bite and swallowed. "I remember you liking him back in the day. It's why you got obsessed with those candies, isn't it?"

"Was I that obvious?"

"No, I'm just good at spotting connections between things. It's what makes me an ace at those escape rooms." She described clues she'd noticed while solving puzzles in escape rooms she'd tried out in Greece and in Ireland. "It was crazy hard to do them in other languages and cultures. Honestly, I didn't win them all. Some cleaned my clock."

We finished our toast, and I got ready for the day. I wore jeans and tall boots, plus an ice-blue fuzzy sweater with a penguin pattern on the front. Ike liked penguins—or at least he had as a younger person.

"I hope you have a good time at the snow sculpture festival."

"You have fun painting." Aunt Gretchen snort-laughed. "You look pretty snazzy for someone who is just going off to paint walls. But don't change a thing," she added quickly. She wrinkled her nose and shook me by the shoulders. "You're so lucky."

"Me!" Little did she know.

"Okay, I take it back."

That was better. Or, was it? "What are you saying?"

"I should have said, *he's so lucky.* Ike is. That a girl as incredible as you, has come into his life. And wearing his favorite animal on your sweater."

Haw, haw. "We're just working on the chapel together. Nothing more."

Aunt Gretchen didn't respond, she just threw a knowing grin over her shoulder as she tugged her Navajo blanket wrap cloak from the coat tree. "Ta-ta!" She disappeared out the door.

I checked myself in the mirror. My cheeks had better color now. I wished I could put my hair in a ponytail, so they'd be more prominent—they were my best feature—but ponytails were for people with two working hands.

It's surprising just how many daily tasks require two hands. I'd been finding that out in a crash course over the past twelve weeks.

There was a stiff knock at the door.

"Hazel?" Ike's voice came through. "Are you ready?"

I opened the door. "I was just heading upstairs. Yesterday kind of knocked me out."

"You're definitely a knock-out." A smile pulled at one side of his mouth. "Penguins." He gazed at my middle but then looked quickly away. "I love penguins."

"Really?" Lie, as if I hadn't known. "Do you want to come in? I still need to …" Okay, I couldn't think of anything I still needed to do, other than have him come inside and talk to me.

"Sure." He gave the apartment a once-over. "It hasn't changed." He stepped in, and his aura filled the whole room. Warmed it. Lightened it.

"Right?" I indicated for him to have a seat, and I sat in the recliner with my feet tucked up under me. "Did you spend much time down here?"

"Your dad made us lunch a few times. You were busy upstairs at the organ. How many hours a week were you practicing, anyway?"

That was one of those things I rarely admitted, since the number would shock anyone who didn't truly dedicate themselves to trying to perfect something that couldn't ever be perfected. "A lot."

"It seemed like all your after-school hours, and late into the night."

"Yeah," I said, not mentioning the hours I spent *before* school every day. "I really wanted to be good." I'd wanted to be the *best.* But that would sound overly ambitious and almost like I was a crackpot. "Anyway, what part are you going to paint today?"

He pressed three fingers to his forehead and rubbed them in a circle. "That's just it. I think—I think I need some time in the fresh air to reset my creative brain."

"By fresh air, do you mean *bracing* air? This is Massey Falls, you know. It's single-digit temperatures today."

"I know, but it's also the snow sculpture festival. Any chance you would want to go?"

Would I!

"With … me?"

Why was he asking it so sheepishly. *Does he think of it as a date?*

My foundations rumbled. Isaac Jacobsen Ivey was *asking me on a date* right this second. And the date would happen instantaneously if I were to say yes.

My heart thrummed in my chest. How much time passed, a second? A minute? Finally, I could talk, and it came out in a tone much more casual and upbeat than the one my brain was shrieking in. "Sure. My aunt was talking about it this morning. When should we go?"

"How's now?"

Now was absolutely great.

***

"Look at that one." The very tall Ike pointed over the heads of all the other festival-goers.

"I can't see it."

"It's right there—oh, you're not tall enough. Here." He hoisted me by the waist, lifting me high enough that I could see a giant hundred-dollar bill carved out of snow, featuring Ben Franklin wearing a Santa hat right in the center.

"I see it." And I felt the strength of his hands and arms at my waist. He placed me back on the ground, but my pulse took a few minutes to regulate. "That was pretty impressive."

We went by several other displays: an ice cream cone, the type of cone with the flat bottom, since a cone-shaped cone would topple if made of snow. There were several snow-sculpted dogs of different breeds, a massive Hello Kitty, a gorilla, a dinosaur, three different robots, even a bouquet of roses with the snow spray-painted red and green.

"People really get creative," he said. We stood next to the food vendor cart, where Ike had ordered us each a crispy churro and a cup of hot chocolate. "What snow sculpture would you want someone to make for you?"

"A swan, but it would be impossible, of course."

"Why so?"

"Because of the neck. The head would topple on something that long and spindly."

He took a bite of his churro. Its cinnamon wafted through the air. "You're probably right."

I bit into the fragrant fried dough stick, and the sugar crunched against my teeth. "These are good."

"She makes the dough fresh." He sipped his cocoa. "And she keeps the cocoa temperature reasonable."

"No cooking ourselves from the inside out?" We strolled a little farther, past a giant koi fish with iridescent scales, a large bust of George Washington, and then we entered Christmas alley, which began with a humongous Frosty the Snowman, the size of a school bus on its end, and it went on from there. "Do you like Christmas?" I asked as we passed a tree the size of the one in Rockefeller Center.

"You'd think I wouldn't anymore, since all the blowback from my family happened, but I still like it. I have the warm memories."

What blowback from his family was he talking about? Should I ask? Would he tell me if I did ask?

"Hazel! Hazel Hollings, is that you?" In less than two seconds, I was engulfed in the hugs of three shrieking women, all jumping up and down and acting like maniacs in the middle of the street. "I can't believe you're here! It's you. We've missed you so much!"

Leela, Bryony, and Natalie all basically mobbed me, asking questions a mile a minute. When they paused to catch their breath, I wasn't sure how to answer. I shot a look at Ike, but he'd gone fully stoic.

"But seriously, Hazel, you're here." Leela's brows pushed together. "You're normally swamped with concerts every afternoon and night during the holidays. Some morning concerts, too, or traveling shows. What's going on?"

Bryony wedged her way in between the two of us, leaning close and lowering her voice. "The bigger question is *are you here with Ike Ivey?* What is going on with you? I thought he was—"

"Gone to medical school?" he interjected. "Yeah, that's the big scandal of my life. Ask Topanga Tycho." He had their full attention. They quit mobbing me and surrounded Ike.

"What *about* you and Topanga? She was gorgeous. Was there an engagement? She always hinted, but we never saw a ring."

A huge snowplow pushed its way down the road, and somehow Ike

45

and I were separated from my three high school friends. While it blocked their view of us, he grabbed me by the left wrist. "Wanna make a run for it?"

I didn't even answer, I started running.

For a few yards, we stayed hidden behind the snowplow, but as soon as there was a large enough tree to dodge behind, we took our opportunity. Soon, we were ensconced in the safe, deep shade of a grove of evergreen oaks.

"Dude, you read my mind."

"That's only because we were thinking exactly the same thing—*scram*."

Scram. Who says that? I couldn't help but smile. "You saved me back there."

"Don't kill me, and don't go bolting off into the blue, but what exactly did I save you from? You tell me, and I can protect you better."

Telling someone? *I don't know.* But telling someone who wants to know to be able to protect me? That was different. Moreover, telling *Ike Ivey* so he could protect me sounded actually like the first safe harbor from the storm my life had become the last three months.

I bit my lower lip and shut my eyes. "I can't play the organ anymore."

"You say that, but I heard you playing it. What do you mean?"

Oh, help me. Please help me. I moved to a spot with a little ray of sun, and Ike followed. In that little ray's light, I removed the mitten from my right hand and exposed its permanently curled feature, the atrophy, the whiff of rigor mortis it displayed.

"It's … useless."

"Oh, Hazel. What happened? Were you in an accident?" Gingerly, he reached out and touched it, taking me by the wrist, turning the hand over, back and forth in the light, inspecting gently. "Are you in pain?"

"You'd think not, since it's so dead. But the pain is pretty unrelenting. There are spikes now and then, but it's mostly a dull throb, day and night."

His soulful blue eyes met mine. "Can you even sleep at night?"

"If I'm tired enough."

"Which means, usually not." He scrunched his nose. "No wonder you've been so easily spooked."

"Is that how you're defining it?"

With the same careful attention as before, he placed the mitten back on me and pulled the sleeve of my coat back down to cover the disappointing sight. "What do the doctors say?"

I just frowned and shook my head.

"What? Bad news? Wait. Don't tell me you haven't even *seen* a doctor."

It was a whole thing, and I couldn't lay all the ugly details on him right then, so I truncated it. "No hand equals no job, and no job equals no insurance."

"Which equals no doctor." He obviously grasped at least a portion of the enormity of my despair. "What can I do to help?"

"Keep my secret." My shame, I could've said. "This isn't a point of pride, necessarily. It's just how disappointed the people in town will be when they find out how massively I've failed them. They were so proud of their favored daughter, the one who *made it* in the city, you know? They invested a lot of emotional capital in me, especially after my dad died. I'm not ready to be in the spotlight of that yet." Ever.

If I could hide the failure forever, I would.

"You can't hide your injury forever."

Injury? Was it an injury? I wasn't sure. "Why not? If I move to another town, change my name, get a job as—I don't know—a crossing guard for elementary school kids I could hide it."

"You don't want that."

"Sure, I do. Er, I might."

"Please, Hazel. I know I said I didn't hear you playing the organ the other day—but when I finally tuned in, I *did* hear you playing. The joy and exuberance of your spirit are still there in the music. You can't deny it. You belong to that medium. It's in your cell structure." He made it sound so romantic.

"I wish there were a way around it, but I've tried everything I can on my own. It hasn't made any difference at all." I couldn't move my fingers more than a millimeter, and doing so induced crazy levels of pain. "I'm washed up as a professional organist, so I need to come to grips with that. For now, I'm still—what did you call it? Easily spooked. But I'll work on that."

Oddly, having told Ike dialed back the freak-out of the whole thing. Of me, I should say. Strange, since I'd assumed talking about it would have had the effect of making it grow even huger. But speaking it aloud had made it seem sort of manageable. At least on an emotional level, if not in other ways.

"Hazel? Don't think I am running away from this topic of conversation—no pun intended—but standing here in these trees has given me about ten flashes of inspiration for the lighting on this one section of my ceiling painting. Would you be okay with going back to the chapel this soon?"

We headed back up the hill, and he reverted to the topic of my hand for a second as we neared the chapel. "If you change your mind, or find a way to pay out of pocket, I know a couple of really good surgeons over at Mendon Regional who could possibly help."

"Thanks. That means a lot to me." If only I had confidence that a medical doctor could do something, but in my heart of hearts, I knew this was not a physical condition. No, it was something a lot deeper. Still, having Ike be so attentive, and so tender, went a long way toward soothing the emotional ache. Did he have any idea how much he'd done to help me, even by just being himself?

That afternoon, I finished reconstructing the rest of the song "Christmas with You" and even got a second ending onto the staff paper. Now that Ike knew about my bum right hand, I didn't bother hiding it up inside the sleeve of my sweater anymore. That relieved some anxiety that I hadn't even noticed was there turning me into a ball of stress. My left-hand-only playing started flowing like an angel's robes in the night wind. I hardly had to think about it at all, and sometimes, I could move it around to play the melody of a song here and there, inserting it while keeping the bass chords going with my feet.

It was actually a little bit fun.

Mercy! I was having fun playing music again! This was amazing. Ike was amazing. No question about it, I was falling for him and his lanky Encyclopedia Brown form, his intelligence, his touch, for his artistic skill, the way he smiled at my lame jokes, the way he helped me escape from uncomfortable situations, the way he brought me ketchup and took my breath away when he lifted me above the crowd to see what only he could see.

But I was falling for him with even more concrete reasons to this time—including the fact he was the sole repository of my secret, and he was determined to protect it. To protect me.

Heaven help me. I was so sunk.

But there was one mystery about him he'd never actually answered: why did he have Dad's sweater? And even more, *why did he wear it every single day?*

During a pause in his work a couple of afternoons later, when I was between ideas on what to play next, I looked up at his progress on the ceiling from my seat at the organ. This was it, my chance. *Why are you wearing the sweater I knitted for Dad today? And every day?*

It was on the tip of my tongue.

"Why are you—" It died in my throat. I couldn't wedge it out from behind my larynx. Instead, what emerged was a far worse question, if less personal to our shared history. "Why are you spending your days painting walls for Mr. Newt when you could be painting something as beautiful as that lost lamb scene?"

His brush clattered onto the platform of the scaffolding and then fell onto the floor. He didn't make a move to pick it up.

Uh. Okay. So apparently *what's a guy like you doing with a simple job like interior painter* turned out to be the wrongest question of all.

Chapter 8

Ike

"You mean you didn't tell her?" Evan Peters, Ms. Eileen's son, had her blunt style of speaking, if not her over-the-top style of everything else. He wore a backward ball cap and sported a three-day mustache. "Why keep the lid on something like that? *If* you want to move things forward with her. You do, right? You always did have a thing for Hazel Hollings. That's obviously why you took the part-time job working with her dad for basically zero pay when we were in junior high."

We were off-loading big bags of foodstuffs from the delivery truck at the community center. The soup kitchen was going to use it for the upcoming holiday meals, and Ms. Eileen had roped Evan into being the muscle. I'd been sucked into the vortex by virtue of being Evan's designated couch-surfer.

"That's not why." I scrunched up my face and pulled away. Wheat flour, rice, beans, pasta, sugar, oats. All fifty-pound bags. They smelled fresh, like they'd come straight from the farmers. I even forgot to feel cold. Maybe that was due to the manual labor, though. "I wanted the experience of doing hard work—so I wouldn't be useless on projects like this one you dragged me out into the cold pre-dawn light to help with."

"Where's your Christmas spirit?"

"It's still in bed. It wakes up around seven."

"You'll survive."

The deflection had worked. Evan started talking about his plans for after his wedding, which was coming up right after Christmas. I listened, mostly, but then he dropped the bomb, detonating it right near my soft spot. "We're moving to Reedsville. Taking off on New Year's Day. You'll have to find a different schmuck's couch."

"When did all this come about?"

"Last week. I told you."

Oh, last week. The first week I'd run into Hazel again. That full-pout lower lip had absorbed all my powers of concentration. "Gotcha," I managed. "I'll find somewhere else to land. Thanks for reminding me."

"I had the feeling you weren't listening when I told you the first time. I get it. When I'm thinking about Cheryl, I'm basically brain dead."

"What does that have to do with—" Never mind. No sense arguing. He totally had me pegged. "Hazel is even better than she used to be."

"I bet. After all these years as a professional, she can only be more skilled at the instrument."

That hadn't been what I'd meant, and Evan knew it. He just grinned. "I know, I know. I saw the two of you walking around together the other day at the hardware store. She seemed to be standing *awfully* close to you. How can you bear it? Are you kissing her yet?"

Kissing her! My back straightened, and I dropped the oats on my boot. "We're just friends. Helping each other out with ..."

Evan gurgled and raised a knowing brow. "Helping each other out can mean a lot of things, pal."

Oh, blash. "Knock it off. She's a really nice girl. A good girl. And I respect her dad too much—and Hazel herself—to compromise that."

"Kissing her isn't compromising her, pal. It's showing genuine feelings. Now, if you *didn't* think she was the most amazing woman you've ever met and you kissed her anyway, that'd be the compromise." He leaned closer to peer at me. "I knew it. You haven't stopped thinking of her as the I Ching."

51

"What does that even mean?" I sort of knew. "Anyway, we're not dating."

Except, we were dating, though, if eating lunch and dinner together every day was dating, and spending all our waking hours together, and only talking to each other most of the time, and texting late into the night was dating. Add to that, my constant stream of thoughts of how I could be the guy she needed. And my wishing she'd someday forgive me for being nothing but the guy who made Loser Choices, a phrase my parents used so often about me they should've started monogramming my shirts with it. "Uh-huh." Evan lifted the final bag onto his shoulder and moved it out to the pile in the brisk morning air that smelled of icy frost and the smoke of wood fires. "Let me know when you propose and what she says."

"Propose. Ha." That … was not happening. Not unless the world fell over on its side and tipped reality upside down. "Not everyone is as *brave* as you are, Evan, my friend. Not everyone has as much to offer a wife." Evan had graduated from law school and was taking a job in the city. "You'll buy a house, pay off your car, buy Cheryl a mini-van, and you'll fill it to the brim with little Peters kids who sing like their Grandma Eileen."

"Like *angels*. Angels who swallowed one of those megaphone speakers."

"Ms. Eileen does like to sing with gusto."

"That's the plan. You should get yourself such a plan."

"I'm a couch surfer. I dropped out of medical school. Women … aren't into that." At least Topanga hadn't been.

"You're only taking Topanga Tycho as your case study. In what ways are Hazel and Topanga the same?"

"They both play the organ at a professional or near-professional level, for one." And for others, they were both beautiful and smart, and daddy's girls, and … the list really went on. We walked over to the table filled with doughnuts and chocolate milk for the volunteers. "Both are top-notch women."

"One of them is top-notchier than the other." Evan pulled off his gloves and swiped at his brow. "Look, you should tell her what happened. That you followed your dream."

"Even though my dream turned out to be a big pile of nothing but an empty savings account and a dead-end job?"

"Even if. And here's why."

This I had to hear. Then I needed to get back to my real job—of prolonging the possibly wrong dream. "Go on. I'm listening."

"Because until you tell her, you won't know how she'll react." He held up a palm to halt my protest, while he grabbed three raised glazed doughnuts with the other. "You think you know, but you don't. Don't pre-judge her. She's grown up different from other people, and she's pretty careful about judging because of it. Think about that."

Much as I didn't want to think about that, or anything else Evan said, it was true that I might need to answer her question about why I was painting for Mr. Newt instead of pursuing the fine arts *like her dad had encouraged me to do.* I zipped my coat higher to keep the cold off Abe Hollings's special sweater and took a few doughnuts of my own.

Evan might be right.

That night, after finishing all the painting of the foliage around the cowboy and the stream—which had only been pencil-sketched in lightly so far—I climbed off the scaffolding. Hazel's organ seat was vacant. I must have been so engrossed in getting the light and shading right on the palm fronds and sagebrush that I hadn't noticed her leaving.

Ach! My aching body. I stretched upward, bent over and touched my toes, and then rolled my neck around to get out the kinks.

"Hazel?" I looked around for her, but she wasn't in the chapel anywhere. With as much as she'd been playing the organ, she might have fallen into a heap at the foot of the bench. "You in here?"

She was gone, and hadn't said goodbye. Bluh. More evidence she wasn't that into me. At least that she wasn't as into me as I was into her. I packed up my things and headed for home.

Over at Evan's place, there was a note on the table. *Gone with*

Cheryl for the cake-tasting. Another perk of proposing. I crumpled the Post-it into a wad and tried tossing it toward the trash can.

The adhesive stuck to my hand, like a sign.

I marched over there and dusted it off my palm.

The doorbell rang. Probably carolers. Some of them came out early in the month, and they probably thought they'd catch Ms. Eileen's son at home. "Evan's not here to—" My words caught in my throat as I swung the door open.

There, in the streaming white rays of the porch light against the black night, stood Hazel. And she was holding a huge plate of the cookies my grandma used to bake, *krumkake*. "Hazel," I said lamely. "You made cookies."

That couldn't have been easy, one-handed.

"Are you going to invite me in?" She shivered and pulled a meek smile. "This is Massey Falls. People who bring cookies get invited in."

"Of course!" I threw the front door open wide and ushered her into the foyer, where she removed her winter boots and set them on the tile.

Then, horror struck. This was no plain old house. It was a bachelor pad, and Evan was engaged, which made him even more useless at keeping things tidy. Wedding invitations and scraps of fabric delivered by Cheryl, plus dirty clothes, pizza boxes, and plastic Solo cups with dried up rings of Pepsi in the bottom were piled high. And that was just the coffee table.

"Welcome to our mess." It was all I had. "Let me move some of these things off the couch." I shoved about a week's worth of laundry, towels, and blankets onto … the floor. "Have a seat."

Great. Now I was the guy who made Loser Choices™ *and* a slob. Nothing about me shouted *Young Man of Promise* here. "Thanks for the cookies. Wow, my grandma's recipe, even."

"How can you tell?"

"From the specks of cardamom." I lifted one to my nose. "Yep, and nutmeg. You got them all so evenly browned."

"I left the burnt ones at home. When Aunt Gretchen was last in

54

Norway, she bought a *krumkake* iron."

"I have an old one you have to set on a gas stove to heat." It was a waffle iron, but round, and flatter, and with a detailed swirly floral pattern on it. "Thank you. I haven't had these in forever."

"Mine's electric. Pretty easy, if you're not a gawky buffalo at it like me." She pulled one off the plate and gave it to me. "You don't make them with your grandma's iron?"

"Never." I crunched the delicate, yellow-brown, crisply lacy edge. "Mmm. That butter!" And the sugar balance and spices were exactly right. How had she done that?

"The recipe called for a whole pound of butter."

"Where'd you get it?"

"From the town recipe book they did as a fundraiser a long time ago. Aunt Gretchen found it in the drawer. It was"—she shrugged and smiled—"your grandma's submitted recipe."

"You sneaky baker!" I took a full bite of the cookie and let it crumble-melt in my mouth. "You nailed these. Trust me. I'm a connoisseur." I offered her one. "Join me?"

She took it and smiled again. That smile crumble-melted *me*. It was a drug. A high-inducing substance I'd gladly use to excess.

"So what do you do when you're not painting walls and ceilings?"

"I keep my apartment tidy and clean as a whistle, obviously."

"Quit being self-conscious about it. I didn't call before I came."

"You brought cookies." I lifted another one from the plate and let its cardamom perfume infuse me with both old memories and present joy. "My other hobby is eating cookies Hazel Hollings makes."

She kicked my ankle lightly. She'd done that back when we were eating burgers the first time I took her to lunch. At the time, I'd assumed it was an accident, a reflex of some kind.

Now? *It's a love tap,* my wishful-thinking brain insisted.

Oh, brother.

"If you're painting as a job, it can't be a hobby is all I was thinking." She tilted her head to the side and chewed. "Or else it becomes a *jobby*."

"Good point." I swallowed both the cookie and my ridiculous train of thoughts. "You promise not to think I'm weird?"

"I already think you're weird."

"I make jam. Especially at Christmas, since there are fewer painting jobs with Mr. Newt."

"But no berries are in season in December."

"No, but there's all the citrus. Orange marmalade is pretty fun to make, and I've done cranberry chutney and apple butter. Kiwis are in season, too. I don't put it in jars usually, just in plastic containers and eat it or give it away. Mostly I eat it or share with Evan." Or whoever's couch I'm borrowing at the time.

Her reaction came on slowly, but it wasn't any form of laughing at me. "That was not even on my radar. But it's so cool. What made you pick that up?"

"Don't get me started."

"No, seriously, I want to know."

If she did, she was in for a ride, because jam was my jam. First, there was the strawberry freezer jam obsession I'd gone through in junior high. "Mom made me take a peanut butter sandwich every day for school lunch, and I got sick of the store jam, and honey was expensive." So I'd made enough jam in the summer one year to last the whole fall semester and into the spring. "After that, I tried blackberry, raspberry, huckleberry. And then came the butters."

For ten whole minutes, Hazel let me wax on about my jam habit. She didn't even look bored. She asked pertinent questions, like whether I used pectin or corn starch.

"Do you want to try some?"

"Do you have some available?" She sat forward. "What flavor?"

"Apple butter. Do you want it on toast?" Soon, we were eating toasty-warm slices of Yuletide Bakery's sourdough bread spread with half an inch of my latest batch of apple butter.

Hazel wiped her mouth with a napkin. Oh, those full lips. "Do you know what I like best about the jam thing?"

"Eating it?" Because that's what I liked, and more or less the sole reason for doing it.

"Hearing you tell me about it. Do you know your eyes light up, and you get this whole glowing excitement? It's gorgeous."

Gorgeous? Me? Oh, she meant the glowing excitement. Hazel couldn't possibly mean she found me interesting physically. "Thanks," I said at last. "That's what you look like when you're sitting at the organ, you know." *Gorgeous.* But she always looked gorgeous, if I was being honest.

"Thanks." She looked at her lap. "I'd better go."

No! I wanted to keep her here. When she was in this apartment, it came to life. "We haven't decorated Evan's tree yet. Look." It stood at the side of the room, leaning sadly against the wall, completely free of decorations. "He's planning his wedding for right after Christmas, and I've been working. Do you have time?"

"I have lots of time. I'm unemployed, remember?" She said it with good humor, not melancholy. *She's making progress out of the dumps.* Was my influence helping? *I wish.*

"Your job is to keep me going at my job. Maybe I should be paying you, but the truth is, all my wages go for one thing—rent."

"Evan is charging you big rent?"

"Not for myself, for my paintings." It was time to crack open that tragic story just a page or two. She'd told me her wonky situation, after all. "They're in storage, and I am pretty protective of them."

"You should be. What is the storage facility like?"

Since she seemed so interested, I—once again—waxed on. I described the climate control, the shelving, the humidity balance. "The frames have to be considered, too, since they're made of wood. It's all a delicate tightrope to walk, since—" I didn't want to sound egotistical about them, so I quit there.

"Since they'll be worth a bunch of money once you get them into the right gallery."

Did this woman have a microscope into my very *soul?* "Um, yeah. Exactly."

"And if it's in the right gallery and one sells—or all of them sell, then what?"

Then, my parents would finally see I hadn't made a Loser Choice™ by listening to advice that came from a different source than them, and that I really could make a living doing art—I'd made a Winner Choice. And I'd trademark *that.*

"It would make my parents proud of me. Possibly." Or at least I could rub it in their faces. Okay, that didn't sound nice, or abounding in holiday spirit. "I want them to believe in me."

"They really should." She sat back against the couch and pulled her knees up to her chest. Her fuzzy socks had pink and phthalo green stripes. She got cuter every time I looked closer. "I mean, I do."

She did? This weird tingling filled my belly—similar to the time I'd left some apple butter at the back of my fridge for a few months and knew it couldn't still be good but I'd eaten it anyway. Fermented. A little drunk on acceptance, maybe.

Should I tell her?

Before I could stop it, the admission came tumbling forth, like she'd pulled the tiny pebble holding back the avalanche. "Your dad believed in me."

"I know."

"Yeah, but he believed in my art. He was the first person to see what I'd been working on, and he said it was good enough. Said I should pursue it." I didn't say the part about choosing art over medical school. Not yet. "When he got sick, he gave me his sweater. I hope you don't mind. It means a lot to me." I wore it every time I painted, or anytime it was cold, just to remind myself that *someone* had once believed.

Hazel leaned her head against the cushion and gave me a doe-eyed look with those intensely blue irises. Which paint would I have to mix to recreate that shade of blue? Two parts french ultramarine, two parts cobalt, one part cerulean, a tiny drop of ivory black …

The way the iris contrasted with the dark ring around it and the white of her eye almost looked like it had been digitally altered, but it was real. Hazel was real. And she sat there, a foot away from me, giving me *that* look, making me feel giddy and alive and sixteen again.

"I wish I could see them sometime."

Oh. All the giddy zings halted. "Um …" I intoned lamely. But I hadn't shown them to anyone. At least not to anyone in Massey Falls. Sure, I'd gone up and down the whole geographical corridor peddling them to gallery owners and getting nothing but shrugs and apologetic faces.

"No pressure," she said. "Just expressing my little wish. You don't have to grant it."

Dang, now I surged with an insane desire to grant her wish—to grant her *every* wish. "I'll show you sometime. How about after I finish the ceiling?"

"Really, it's fine."

"No, I want to." I wanted to show her the art I'd created. I wanted to show her my whole heart. *How she sees the art is how she will see me.*

Okay, not actually. But I wished she could accept the art, and the jam, and the bits of me that I had been keeping behind locked doors ever since I'd made those Loser Choices™ and tanked my life, according to those who knew and loved me best.

"After you finish the ceiling would be great. If you're feeling like it."

When I was around Hazel, I felt all kinds of unexpected things.

One of them might be *falling in love.*

"I hope the right gallery owner discovers you." She gave me a soft smile.

"Thanks. Me, too. Maybe it'll happen this Christmas. He's coming, you know, to the candle lighting service. And he's opening a gallery, they say, Western art, even."

"Who's coming? A gallery owner? I thought Ms. Eileen said she was inviting that, um, other arts promoter who shall not be named."

She didn't want to namedrop Trey Tycho? That made a few things that had happened during her freak outs a couple of weeks ago make more sense. But she might as well know the truth, so as not to be blindsided on the night of the candle lighting service. "The person opening the Western art gallery *is* Trey Tycho."

Her face went from blushing pink to sickly pale. Naturally, she had to leave. Immediately.

Chapter 9

Hazel

I pounded my head down onto my folded arms. "I'm such an idiot, Aunt Gretchen! There we were, having the best time ever. And I swear—he was into me." It had been as if he'd forgotten Topanga Tycho even existed, whether she was still in his life or not. "He wasn't just messing with me. He kept touching me like he couldn't help himself, and he sat so close to me on the couch I couldn't even stretch out my legs. Then I had to go and ruin everything by getting all emotional *again*. I'm letting myself be completely controlled by my past."

We were riding in Aunt Gretchen's rental SUV toward the toy store, where she had arranged for all the donations from fundraising for her humanitarian trips to be spent on toys to take to her next location. It was, she said, the least she could do for the local economy of the town that had raised and launched her life.

"What exactly *did* happen in your past that you're letting it have such sway over you now? You've told him at least some part of it, I gather." We had parked in the lot behind the toy store. "More than you've told me?"

"I guess so." Wow, I hadn't even shared with my closest relative as much as I'd spilled to Ike. "Do you *want* to know?" Since she did, I told her—everything, from the moment of the injury to the firing to the slinking away from my world in ignominy.

"Well, that's just persecution!" Gretchen pulled at her two curl-springing pigtails in solidarity. "Are you kidding me right now? I'm going to wring that man's neck if I ever see him in person." Her phone rang just then, and she answered in a shockingly pleasant voice, following the shrill reaction to my tragic tale she'd just voiced.

To avoid listening in on her professional call, I climbed out of the car. But before I could walk into the back door of the toy store, Aunt Gretchen rolled down her window and covered the receiver on her phone. "You have to tell him, sweetie. And the sooner the better."

I stood there with snowflakes falling on my face and eyelashes and hair, knowing inside and out that she was right.

It was time.

***

"I recognize that piece." Ike was perched on his scaffolding a couple of hours later that afternoon, and he peered over the edge of it at me. "It's Bach, right? 'Toccata and Fugue in D Minor.'"

It was a famous piece, but not everyone knew it by name. They just called it *that one song from horror films*. But what was weird was the fact Ike could recognize it by the left hand alone, considering most of the movement came from the right hand.

"You are correct." I was too nervous to give him much more than that. If I were going to tell him something as shatteringly humiliating as the whole story surrounding my injury, I needed fortitude, which I was lacking, like the roll of tape or the sharp scissors whenever it was urgently time to wrap a present. "How's your painting going?"

"I'm just finishing the pale beiges of the desert floor behind the action scene."

"But you haven't done the river yet? Or the figure or the animal?"

"It's coming. Soon. It has to." He sounded as nervous as I felt, and suddenly, my past didn't seem to contain quite as much pressure as his future. After all, mine had already happened, and I knew the outcome.

It was just weird that both of our careers seemed to hinge on the approval of the very same person, the recently crowned king of the arts world in the entire region, Trey Tycho.

Thinking his name made me miss some notes, and I ended up pressing the wrong chords entirely, ten in a row. Yeah, it was time to get this out of my system.

"Just a wild guess," Ike said from above, "but do you need to talk about something? Can I take you to the waterfalls? I need more fresh air again."

***

At the waterfall for which the town of Massey Falls was named, Ike helped me out of his work truck. He stood close to me as we walked down the narrow trail toward the top of the falls. Bare tree branches each had individual lines of freshly fallen snow atop them, except for those with winter chickadees perched atop their narrow rods. The trail itself was popular and had been well-trodden all winter, so only the most recent inch or so of snow covered its caked-mud and stones. Yes, it was narrow, but it was wide enough for two people walking side by side. The roar of the falls grew louder as we made our way closer.

"Watch out for that boulder." Ike stood at my right, and he hooked my elbow, pulling me closer to him so I wouldn't catch my foot on the protruding rock. "Give me your other hand."

I took my good hand from my coat pocket, and he whipped off my mitten and laced his fingers through mine. "That will make it easier to keep you safe."

The pressure of his hot palm against my cold one spread heat like wildfire through my veins. How long had it been since I'd held hands with a man? High school? Yeah, it was just the once at that big statewide music competition in the state capital, and one of the other musicians had selected me as his crush-of-the-week, and we'd held hands during the dance the last night of the competition.

I didn't even remember his name.

But I'd never forgotten Ike.

Ike's hands were strong and rough from the manual labor he did, but I also knew they managed precision and tenderness with equal dexterity. *I'm in love with this guy's hands.* They were the strongest things I'd ever felt.

"Look. The falls." He helped me navigate one last trail-hazard, a fallen tree limb, and then we settled onto the angle of a flat-sided boulder. "I come up here to think sometimes."

"Everyone in town does, sooner or later. Or else they come up here to make out. It's more or less the fabled *inspiration point*." If I hadn't been holding Ike's hand at that moment, I would have clapped a palm over my mouth. How could I mention *making out* right here in front of him, right now, while we were *at* so-called inspiration point?

My awkwardness once again knew no bounds.

"You inspire me," Ike said, rescuing me. "But of course you already know that. Without your help, none of my artwork in the chapel would've come to life. Thank you, Hazel." He gazed down at me with those soulful blue eyes, and I felt their searching all the way to my toes, and I thought if I couldn't kiss him I'd go crazy. "Honestly, I owe you so much."

Pay me in kisses. I licked my lips and then bit my lower one. "It's the least I can do."

"What have I done for you?" He gave a single syllable laugh. "Well, besides the obvious—bringing you little paper cups of ketchup for your fries."

He'd done so much more than he knew. He'd made my injury seem less all-encompassing. "You've been my confidant." I steeled myself and went on. "Speaking of confidants, there's more I need to tell you, so you'll know why I'm *still* so easily spooked." I clenched my teeth together for a second for strength. "Are you okay with hearing what comes next?"

He volleyed a version of my past phrase right back at me. "You can tell me anything."

And so I did. I told him anything. Everything.

There I was in the vast new Center for Arts auditorium, playing the second-to-last song in the global choir festival in Reedsville. Six hundred combined voices from nineteen countries, hand-selected through rigorous auditions conducted by the producer himself.

One organist.

An audience had tuned in live from all four quarters of the earth. A massive swell came at the top of the final page, and without warning, I felt a sharp pain in my brain, shattering. Blinding. And then—my right hand painfully seized up. The fingers curled into their current position. I flubbed the notes, but I kept going with my left hand and the pedals. The right hand was now useless. The director gave me a fix yourself up or die now *look, and kept leading. The tenors, who could see my hands from their position on the risers, gave me desperate and pitying looks.*

With zero grace, I managed to finish the song with some clunkers, but for the last song, the finale, I couldn't even begin it. My head was splitting, my ears ringing, and the sting in my hand was unbearable. Tears poured down my cheeks, and if I'd worn a dress of any other color but black, it would've looked sopping wet. I slunk off the bench, kicked off my organ slippers and put on my regular shoes. I made it down the steps and off the dais, out the door, before I crumpled to a heap.

Seconds later, the producer appeared, his face as red as velvet ribbons, and his eyes as black as Frosty's coal buttons, with their fury all directed at me.

He told me I'd ruined ten months of preparation. That I was the biggest disappointment of his career. That I was, naturally, fired. But also that he would make sure I'd never work in the field of music ever again, and that he would be seeing me in court, suing me for damages, including the airfare for six hundred musicians flown in from all over the globe.

At that point, he'd bent down and gotten right in my face and said ... some other things I didn't want to think about even now. But they involved his daughter Topanga, and her undisputed superiority to me in every conceivable arena.

"What you needed was the paramedics, not a lecture!" Ike was looking directly at me with an intensity I'd never seen before in a human being, even from him. His eyes had welled up—and of course mine were spilling everywhere—my curse. "I can't believe the producer of the show did that to you. That's the most insensitive thing I've ever heard of, kicking a woman when she's just had a severe medical event. It's wrong. Where is he? I could just wring his neck." He disconnected our grip and mimed wrapping his fingers around an invisible throat.

"There's no need to resort to violence, Ike." It was a sweet gesture, if falling on the side of brutality. It was just nice to think that someone was as upset for me, or even more so, as I had been for myself.

"I'm not violent by nature, but I could seriously become so—for you. Oh, Hazel." He wrapped his arms around me, pulling me tight against his chest. My ear pressed against his ribcage, and his heart was thrumming like the little drummer boy's steady beat, but in cut-time.

Or maybe that was my own pulse, skyrocketing.

"Hazel," he offered my name again, and on his lips, it almost sounded like a prayer. He pushed back, and then he cupped both sides of my face, tilting it upward, and in a swift, decisive, powerful movement, he dipped down and pressed his lips to mine.

My eyes shut, and I succumbed to his insistent request.

This was no doubt-laden, unconfident motion. It was a declaration of possession. His kiss took me by storm, owning me with every sweep and wave. It was the finale of a soaring Tchaikovsky overture, complete with cannons and tympanis and brass.

For the first kiss of my life, I'd never expected anything to be quite so encompassing, so engrossing, so soul-defining. *He's marking me as his own with this kiss, imprinting on my very being.*

I reached around and placed my palms against his back, pulling him closer, and for a split-second, I noted that as soon as his lips met my own, my hand hadn't hurt. Oh, that it could last all day, that it could last forever.

I'm being healed by his touch, his tenderness, his kiss.

Chapter 10

Ike

Kissing Hazel. I was kissing Hazel Hollings. All my years-long, pent-up desire for this incredible woman I lavished on her in those moments at the waterfall where I'd always dreamed of taking her for our first kiss. The splashing and roaring of the falls went silent as my senses all absorbed into one, riveting focus: *kiss Hazel. Show her she is the painting emblazoned on my heart and in my mind and soul.* Every pass of her lips over mine was like a sweep of a paintbrush laden with iridescent, infinitely diverse paints, sparkling and new and bringing light and life to every cell, every atom inside me.

She'd been hurt, and yet she gave so much to me of herself. I craved with an insane need to do anything I could to heal her in return. This kiss, these kisses, had to be showing her how deeply I ached to be her protector and her connection to hope and love.

Hazel crushed me to her, and the intensity between us soared. I had to be nearer to her. I needed us to meld, like mixing two shades on my palette and becoming something altogether new—her soul's winsor blues and my soul's alizarin crimsons combining to make deep violet. Maybe even ultraviolet. It was ultra something, for sure.

The kiss took over coherent thoughts. I lifted her up and placed her higher against the boulder, leaning over her to give her the kisses that had lain dormant inside me for her, for only Hazel, for ages. Maybe for forever.

Thunder clapped, and she pulled away, glancing toward the sky. "It's raining. Did you notice?"

How could I have? I'd gone to another dimension, the cosmos of kissing Hazel. "Should we go?" It was all I could do not to lift her and carry her all the way back to the truck, as if over a threshold. Because it did seem we'd entered new territory. That kiss had, at least for me, started a new life.

If I hadn't fallen a hundred percent in love with her before now, I was dangerously close after that magic-laden experience.

"Ike, that was ..." She seemed to be catching her breath.

"Yeah, it was." There were no adjectives. Only colors and light could convey what that connection had been. "I'm falling for you," I lied. I already had.

She stopped on the trail near a holly tree, which pulled me to a stop as well, since our hands were locked together. Her eyes sparkled, as if full of tears—one of the many endearing things about her. Not everyone could express emotion so readily. What a gift.

"Are you all right?" I asked.

"While you kissed me, my hand didn't hurt."

"Then I should do it more often."

"You should." A little wry smile lifted both sides of her beautiful mouth. "As often as possible."

She didn't have to invite twice. We kissed once more right then and there on the trail, in the gentle rain. And then, I actually did lift and carry her back toward the truck, her legs dangling over my arm. She pressed little kisses against my jaw line and throat as we went. It was all I could do to keep moving, thanks to the distraction. When we got to the truck, I placed her inside and kissed her for another couple of moments before another car pulled up, a mini-van full of children.

Halfway back to town, she slid toward me and rested her head against my shoulder—which was ten times better than when she'd rested her hand on it the other day. I could've driven to the coast and back without stopping if she'd have just stayed there. Time erased itself, and it became just the two of us, connected and safe and the only reality that mattered.

At the doors of Falls View Chapel, she paused and looked up at me, which I took as an opening and kissed her again. There, my brain's synapses crackled to life. This time, not just with desire or connection, but with a heretofore unknown explosion of images—picture after picture of what I could paint or draw or sculpt in the future burst into my mind's eye. And I didn't even sculpt. There were deserts and landscapes and animals and foliage and all the things my soul longed to bring to life through art, things that had possibly always been inside me, locked in some kind of tightly sealed box, but Hazel's affectionate acceptance of me served as the golden key to not only unlock it, but to blow the lid off the hinges and unleash all the rays of illuminating bliss.

How could her touch be so powerful?

A voice from deep inside the box answered with a whispered truth. *Love is the most powerful thing in the universe. Never forget.*

My knees almost buckled. The wind blew a sprinkling of icy snow crystals against my cheek, as if nature punctuated the pronunciation of the voice of truth.

"We should get to work." I held the door for her, and she gave me a shy but loving smile. "Once I finish the ceiling, I have some ideas for more paintings."

"You do?" She followed me into the chapel, and it took all my willpower to leave her and climb the scaffolding. "I'm sure they'll be magnificent."

Yes, that was exactly the adjective for the ideas I'd seen spring forth from the box in my mind during Hazel's potent kiss.

She sat at the organ and picked out a few notes. She was improving. It was amazing how much melody she could create, despite her physical challenge. It inspired me almost as much as her kiss. With the power of love surging all around me, I began work on the horse and rider. The stream was already in place. By the next week, I would be ready to add the final element—the little black sheep in distress against the violent flow of the stream.

Yes, what a relief. My back pressed against the length of the platform on the scaffolding, and I absorbed the music from Hazel's playing, completely at peace, until ...

You dolt! Love isn't just receiving. Ouch. My brain was so right. I couldn't just *take* from Hazel. I needed to figure out some way to make her situation better.

While I mixed the burnt sienna and the raw umber, along with a touch of cadmium red and yellow ochre, on my palette for the horse's flank, the music continued, all from her left hand, and ...

I knew! I knew exactly what to do.

The horse practically painted itself, and when its neck and hindquarters and legs appeared in full-form, it was time to quit painting for the day and get started on something much more lasting.

"I'm heading out." I descended the metal rungs and landed with a jump, both feet on the wood floor. "Do you want to grab dinner with me?"

From her spot on the bench, Hazel looked up. "Don't take this wrong, but today I'm not quite ready to leave. I have this ... idea."

She had an idea! Maybe the kiss had inspired in her a similar creative stroke of genius as it had in me. "That's fine. I can bring you something, if you like." *I'll be bringing her something tomorrow morning, no matter what. Just not food.* "Unless you need to keep concentrating, and I get that."

Hazel tilted her head to the side and bestowed on me the most beautiful smile. "You do get it. I'll see you tomorrow then?"

"Tomorrow." And I practically loped out the door and sped like a maniac down the twisty road of the hill toward town.

Back at Evan's place, he was there, eating Spaghettios straight from a pot. "Hey, you're back early. And I see you decorated the tree. It looks good, but why do it? Never mind. I think I know." He took another bite, and I peered into his makeshift bowl. It was Chef Boyardee's finest offering—the Spaghettios *with* franks. "Don't make that face at my gourmet meal. You know you love it, too."

"Can I use your printer?"

"It might be out of paper, but sure. What's up?"

"I need to print something." My phone was already connecting to the device, and I sent the command for it to give me what I'd selected on my screen—something that had taken much less time to hunt up than I would've expected, and only cost me a few shillings, thank goodness. The choice of music had been easy once I phoned Ms. Eileen, who gave me the correct list.

"Obviously." He took another big spoonful as the sheet music exited the machine and lay face-up on the tray. "Don't tell me, it's for Hazel Hollings. What sheet music could she possibly need that she doesn't already have?"

I swiped the pages up from the tray and held them close to my chest. The title "Silent Night" was normal enough, but the subtitle at the top of the piece announced another important fact. "Arranged for Left Hand Only."

Well, the music was for piano, not for organ, and not arranged personally for Hazel, like I would've wished. No, it wasn't perfect, but it was an approximation. Would she accept it?

"Ike, dude." Evan's spoon scraped the bottom of the pot with a metallic clang. "Please tell me you've come clean with her about the truth of your situation."

"Which truth is that?" My head was full of visions of Hazel's face when I gave her the stack of papers in my arms, of the way her eyes would dance, the way her cheeks would blush and how she'd shower me with her exquisite kisses. "She already knows I'm a failed painter, and she doesn't care." But not for long. Not with her influence and the opportunity Ms. Eileen had provided me.

"Um, but there's more. Remember? The whole *dropping out of medical school* part."

"Yeah, but that's obvious. I'm not a doctor."

"But you have the debts of one. You borrowed three and a half years' worth of tuition money that has to be repaid, my friend."

His words clanged louder than the spoon in the pot as he threw them both into the sink. "Oh." I staggered to the recliner, not bothering to move all the clean laundry off it. "It's in deferment."

"But that doesn't mean it's erased."

"Got it, Captain Obvious."

"Hey, I'm just looking out for you, as a friend. You can't conceal something as enormous as that from a woman who you have ... *feelings* for, you know? That's fraud."

"Thanks, counselor." Dang lawyers.

Blash.

Blash, blash, blash!

Evan was too right for his own good. Or, rather, mine.

How could I have let something so key to whether I'd be a good protector for her get buried in my consciousness? Or the deep reason why Topanga had kicked me to the curb when I announced I was leaving medical school to pursue art?

"Okay, okay. You're right. Thanks." Sort of thanks. Not really. It stung like sparks off the yule log. "Is your fiancée okay with your student debt? What did she say when you slammed her with those numbers?"

"I've got a job at a firm lined up."

Ah, therein lay the difference between Evan and me. He had a potential income, and ...

Unless I get picked up by Trey Tycho for his gallery, I can't possibly offer myself as Hazel's anything.

The printout crumpled in my fist.

Chapter 11

Hazel

Ike was late this morning. It was fine. Right? Just that now that I'd kissed him and he'd kissed me, an invisible thread of gold connected us, and mine stretched out to find him day and night.

And morning, apparently. I sat at the organ's bench and tried over and over to play. Lately, it had been easier, and since the kiss, the fingers of my right hand had been less stiff. Still unusable, but less painful.

I'd take whatever wins I could get, believe me. They were all thanks to things that had transpired right here in this very room. Ike, and me, and the ceiling, and this musical instrument. We were all blending together in some kind of cosmic healing process. Not a completed one, obviously, but there had been improvement. They said that happiness was directional. For the first time in ages, I knew for sure I was heading in a happy direction.

Just then, my fingers and feet lost communication with each other and clunked out a discordant note. At the same time, my mind hollered, *You haven't told Ike that the show's producer was Trey Tycho.*

Um, yeah. While that would never matter in normal life and with anyone else, I knew the truth: Ike's whole future depended on the patronage of Trey Tycho.

If Ike were connected to me, Tycho's biggest nemesis and disappointment—based on the man's own shouted words—then Ike's chances for future art success sank like a rock. My devastating secret and wretched past lay like treacherous rocks near a harbor to destroy Ike—and us. It had already wrecked the ship of my own career. He needed to know.

But I'm not ready to lose him. Not when we just found each other after my wanting him for so, so long.

The back doors of the chapel flung wide, and my head whipped that direction. *Ike!* His entry had to be a sign that it was time for me to tell him the whole truth right now.

"Well, if it isn't Hazel Hollings."

Not Ike.

Topanga? Topanga Tycho? What was *she* doing here? Well, besides strutting toward me with the same snotty air she always wore around me, her hair still in perfect blonde piles of waves, but updated to the latest trend, and wearing the classiest expensive trousers and silk shirt. Never less than perfection, of course.

"Hi, Topanga." I mustered my manners. We were in a chapel, after all. God was probably watching. "What are you doing in Massey Falls? I thought you were working for your dad in Reedsville."

"Like you used to?" Topanga strode up the aisle between the pews toward me. "Before Dad fired you for the disgrace you brought on everyone?"

Retreading worn-to-bedrock ground, thanks. "What do you want?" *Please say you're not here to reclaim Ike.* I'd never discovered with clarity whether he still had any commitment to Topanga. For a brief moment, my heart clutched with doubts.

"I want time on that organ to practice."

Was that all? I practically slumped with relief.

She went on, "You have hogged it for years, Hazel. Rent-free."

How would Topanga know about the arrangement between Dad and Ms. Eileen—that he and I could live in the basement of Falls View Chapel and I could practice anytime day or night, while Dad served as the caretaker of the property? That was no one else's business. Of course, Topanga had her ways of figuring out everyone's business. How could I forget?

"It's yours, but why? You have the Reedsville Fine Arts Hall anytime *you* want. That's a much bigger instrument. Trust me, I know. I played it for years."

"Until you weren't allowed to set foot on the property anymore, by order of the courts, you mean."

Salt, meet wounds. "I'm glad you're here, Topanga." And extra glad Ike wasn't here in this moment. "Merry Christmas." I slid off the organ bench and waved my clenched right fist over it, from pipes to keyboard to pedals while I put my shoes back on. "All yours."

"Thank you. Finally."

Rude. Whatever. I stepped aside and headed up the aisle to make way, and Topanga flicked off her high-heeled patent-leather pumps, climbed onto the bench, and began testing out the keys. She'd always been just two steps behind me since she started later in life, but I couldn't fault her for the skills she'd worked to acquire. Professional courtesy demanded I admire what anyone could do with the complex instrument that combined wind and wood and metal to create timeless music.

Something made me stop and turn back as I reached the door. She'd paused in her playing so I asked, "But again, why? Why this instrument, and why now?"

Topanga gave me that sickly sweet smile of hers, the one she used at her most insincere moments. "Because I'm going to step up and play the organ for the candle-lighting service here on Christmas Eve."

But—but! "But, Ms. Eileen requested that I play on Christmas Eve."

"You told her no. She knew I was attending with my dad, so she reached out. You snooze you lose." She played a menacing minor chord. "And when Ike hears my music, he'll forget all about you. *Again.* Just like before."

"Why would you want him? Didn't you dump him?" It was a shot in the dark. No one had told me so, but if I were wrong, Topanga would for sure set me straight right now. "Or now that he's a rising star in the art world are you slinking back to him?"

"I am slinky, aren't I? It's one of my most alluring characteristics. Men can't resist it—because they don't want to."

She was so ridiculous.

She laughed like she knew that fact but didn't care. "Oh, get off your prudish high horse, Hazel. I'm here because I heard that Ike is more of a genius than any of us ever supposed. And I had that confirmed when I walked in just now and saw the work he's doing on the ceiling of this chapel. Good discovery, girl. And you'll step aside from Ike, just like you stepped aside from the organ just now." She waved goodbye fingers at me, then turned back to playing. She chose a complex fugue that could only *ever* be played with two hands.

I backed out of the room and ran down the steps to the apartment, where Aunt Gretchen met me at the door. "Is that your music? Is it a recording? I haven't heard you play with that much vigor this whole time you've been home. Oh, right." She looked down at my hand and got that same sick, pitying look as always. "Who is it? Who's playing?"

"It's Topanga Tycho. She's going to accompany the congregation for the Christmas Eve services."

Aunt Gretchen's lips pushed to one side. "Well, you did tell Ms. Eileen no."

I crumbled and groaned loudly. "I know! And I should've said yes, even though I can't do it. If only to keep Topanga from—"

"From what? Stealing your man again?" She broke into a laugh. "Not possible."

If that's what Aunt Gretchen thought, she didn't know much about Topanga Tycho.

I grabbed a pint of ice cream from the freezer and set it on the table, ready to dig in, but the lid was stuck. Without both hands, I couldn't even get to my wallowing-food. I let out a primal whimper. Aunt Gretchen came over and opened the container for me and brought me a spoon. "There's a solution, you know. You *could* still play for Christmas Eve."

"How?"

"I don't know."

"Thanks."

"You'll find a way. Maybe Ike can help."

A knock came on the doorjamb of the open door. "How can I help?" Ike stepped into the room. "Is everything okay?"

Aunt Gretchen grabbed her Navajo blanket coat and slipped up the stairs with a quick goodbye. Ike came in and sat down beside me at the table.

"How's my girl this morning?"

"You're late."

"I had something to do. I'm getting you a present."

"You are?" The word present lifted some of the gloom. "I wasn't expecting that." I should get him something, too, but the real thing I needed to give him was the truth about my big disaster, and explain how detrimental it could end up being for him—so that he could make an informed decision between me and Topanga. "Thank you. What is it?"

"You'll see. I thought it would be ready this morning, but it wasn't. I heard music as I came in, but it didn't sound like you, so I came straight downstairs."

That must have been his way of obliquely asking who was playing the organ. I bit my lips together for a second before releasing the Kraken. "It's Topanga. She's going to play for the candle-lighting ceremony."

"She is?" His brow quirked. His cheeks reddened. Some kind of goofy fluttering took over his eyelids. "Huh."

Huh? That was his whole reaction? Nothing conciliatory to soothe me? No pep talk?

My heart flung up and down like a yo-yo from a kid's Christmas toy pile—a kid who didn't know how to use it well and it swung up only once before hitting the floor with a clatter.

"You're probably wondering why I headed down here instead of to my scaffold. I heard that Ms. Eileen is in the hospital, and I thought we should visit. Take her flowers or something."

"Ms. Eileen? But I thought it was her daughter-in-law who was going to be in the hospital, giving birth. What happened? Who's taking care of the other kids?" My own problems shrank instantly. "Let's go."

We climbed into his work truck and he took us in the direction of Mendon. Its regional hospital was the best option for childbirth, and for any serious problems. Far better than the urgent care clinic we had in Massey Falls. Mendon had surgeons and obstetricians and diagnosticians on staff, from what I'd heard. Good ones, too.

Ike explained Ms. Eileen's crisis—emergency appendectomy. She'd thought the pain was from lifting a toddler wrong, but it didn't go away, so her son-in-law took her in to be checked.

"Evan and his fiancée Cheryl have gone to Mendon to be with the kids while their mom and grandma recover."

"That's nice. He's a good son and brother." I was glad for the change of topic, but I still needed to tell him about what I'd done wrong. "I want to be good like that, even though I don't have parents or siblings."

"You are, you know. Your dad was always so proud of you. When he gave me his sweater, I knew it was his prized possession."

"Yeah?" Thoughts of my problems fled at Ike's words. "When did he give it to you?"

"I guess it was kind of a token so I could be brave. It was right after I decided to drop out of medical school but before I'd actually, you know, pulled the trigger on that."

"Had I already gone to Reedsville by then?"

"Yeah. He was pretty sick, but he said he believed in me and that I should follow what my gut told me was the right move for my future. *And my heart.*"

The blood raced in my veins, sparkling like the sun on a snowfield.

"And was it?" It came through my constricted throat, tight from memories of Dad, and getting some kind of supernatural sense that Dad had always wished Ike and I could have some time together in this life, whether for a short or a long amount of time. Dad had his problems, but I loved him anyway, and his opinions and ability to judge character still guided me, over the last five years without him.

Ike reached over and touched my wrist, squeezing it softly and staying silent for a few miles. I couldn't speak either. The moment was too precious to mar with bad revelations. When we parked behind Mendon Regional, he leaned over and kissed me softly.

"I have made a lot of mistakes. You're not one of them."

His words turned me into a slice of chocolate cake being doused with hot ganache, warm and sweet and enclosed in safety. No, I hadn't given him the truth, but he might not hate me for it when I did. Right?

Inside the hospital, we found Ms. Eileen's post-op room. The air zinged with antiseptic and the efficiency of the medical staff. Ike said hello to her, and then whispered softly in my ear.

"I'm heading to the gift shop to grab some flowers. She doesn't have any pink daisies and they're her favorite."

"Gotcha." I leaned up against his shoulder one last time and then came and sat down beside Ms. Eileen. I'd never seen her without a half dozen necklaces, but maybe all the tubes going into her arm and the EKG cords taped to her chest counted. They were a little bit colorful.

"You saw Topanga, I take it?" Ms. Eileen sat up heavily and tossed a bit before getting comfortable. "I should've let you know she was coming. And I was going to, but then this darn thing happened to me."

"Don't worry about that." I shifted my weight with the pressure of what my soul was exploding to say. "So, Ms. Eileen, if it's okay, I'd like to change my mind."

"About?"

"About playing for the candle-lighting service." There! I'd done it! I'd been the bravest musically that I'd been since returning to Massey Falls, other than taking my seat on the organ bench again at all. "I don't know how well it will go, but I'm happy to do it."

"Oh, honey." Ms. Eileen touched her heart, her hospital gown gaping at the armpit. "That ship has sailed. You were so firm about rejecting my offer that I went ahead and signed a performance contract with Topanga Tycho. It's a done deal, sweetie. Take comfort in the fact you were my first choice, of course, but there's nothing I can do at this point."

My face must have been the most readable thing in the universe.

"It's a shame, for sure. However, that composition from Jesse Parrish, written just for you, is sitting on my dining room table, and I'll bring it to you personally the second they let me out of this prison." She still didn't know about my inability to play it. Should I tell her now? She cut me off. "Meanwhile, it seems like things are going well with you and Isaac." Her eyes twinkled. "Tell me about that?"

I just smiled, and then Ike came in and presented her with the flowers, told her he was nearly done with the ceiling and couldn't wait for her to see it.

"I'm determined to be there for the candle-lighting service, my dear ones. Send up a few prayers for me to heal fast enough?"

We promised and then her doctor came in, so we took off.

As we left and headed down the hallway toward the exit, Ike pointed a thumb at one of the closed doors. "That's my friend Jasher's office." The nameplate read *Jasher Hotchkiss, MD*. "We met in medical school as fourth years, but he went on and specialized. He's great with knee surgery."

An air of wistfulness swirled.

I did some quick math. If Ike had known this Dr. Hotchkiss as a fourth year, and if Dr. Hotchkiss was already a surgeon, then, Ike had been in school longer than I thought. Somehow, it had not occurred to me that Ike had been a med student for that long. Wow, he'd nearly become a doctor. And then, Dad had steered him in another direction.

Had Dad done the right thing?

If not, then *two* Hollings family members were likely the ship-sinking rocks for Isaac Ivey. Not that Ike seemed to see it that way. He was holding my left hand as he drove, running his thumb across the sensitive area of my inner wrist. I couldn't get enough of that, couldn't get enough of Ike.

Which was why I really had to come clean.

"Ike? What are your Christmas traditions?" I asked instead, being the world's crawlingest coward that I was. "Does your family have any?"

"Dinner the Saturday before Christmas, with extended family and cousins at my parents' house. Big shindig with turkey and pies and the kids doing the nativity play in bathrobes. The works."

That sounded amazing. "I've never had a big family gathering like that. Do you go every year?"

"Used to. But I haven't for a few."

I wasn't blind. "As in, five years?" Since the time he dropped out of medical school. Quick math raced through my brain again. Something must have gone horribly awry between him and his family when he dropped out. A parent would've been pretty upset.

"Five," he confirmed, his lips pressing into a grim line. "I miss it." He turned toward me. "Would you—do you want to experience it? For you, Hazel, I'd at least put my hatchet under the woodpile, even if I couldn't bury it completely."

"But I'm the daughter of the man who convinced you to follow your gut."

"Yeah." With his free left hand, he gripped the wheel and flexed his fingers and gripped it again. "But if we're going to be together, we have to face up to all the hard things. Together."

Together. The word was a warm fireplace, with a cup of mulled cider and a soft blanket.

Now I really didn't want to tell him about my history with Trey Tycho to spoil the moment. He'd have to know. Soon.

"I'd love to go with you to your family's Christmas dinner."

Ike needed to mend fences with them, somehow, and if there was a way I could help—and not hurt it—I wanted to be part of that healing. Just like he'd been the reason mine had begun.

"Good. Because there is something I really need to tell you."

"Tell me now?" I asked, my heart a snow globe's glitter, all fluttering around me.

"Oh, yeah. Anyway, I want to, but we're at the chapel, and we both need to get to work today." He glanced toward the spot where Topanga's car had been parked.

What did he have to tell me? *Please say it's not about his enduring love for Topanga Tycho. That he's not going to try to let me down easy.*

Chapter 12

Ike

S o, no. I hadn't exactly spelled out to Hazel the enormity of my student debt, but I'd hinted at it. She'd picked up on the hint, right?

That little white lie delivered its venom a few times as I drove to Falls View Chapel to pick her up. My necktie was too tight. My shoulders had broadened from manual labor since the last time I'd worn the sport-coat required for holiday dinner dress at Casa de Ivey. That, or I was feeling all tied up in knots no matter what.

Dinner with them after so long. Dinner with them *and* Hazel, who—as always, so incisive—pinpointed the main complaint my parents could latch onto when they met her, that her dad had been responsible for the demise of my medical career.

Which, totally wasn't accurate. I'd been the one who'd chosen. Not him. He'd only said, *Ike, you're a painter. Your soul won't have time to express itself again for another however-many years if you complete medical school. Is that what you want? To be bottled up for decades?*

Two statements and two questions. That's all he'd done to, as Mom claimed, derail my life and entice me into making the main Loser Choice™, which had, of course, led to the second Loser Choice™ of missing out on Topanga Tycho.

Sure, Topanga had a lot going for her. She even played the organ, which had made her, weirdly, a substitute for Hazel when I'd schooled myself into believing Hazel herself was beyond my grasp and had quit dreaming of her.

But Topanga had been a mere shadow, a flicker on the cave wall, compared to the real substantial woman I now allowed myself to hope would love me.

I pulled up at the chapel, and she was waiting outside for me. Her eyes were bright, but her expression mirrored my own: pure trepidation.

It hit me—what if one of my parents or family members asked Hazel to perform on the piano this evening, possibly out of a resurrected urge to compare Hazel to Topanga. This time around, Hazel might come up short, considering the injury. But she'd sworn me to secrecy about it, so I wouldn't be able to explain, or to defend her.

Well, I'd keep her secret anyway. I'd be what she needed, no matter what.

"Are you ready to go into the lions' den?" I helped her into the passenger side of my old car. The work truck was parked for the weekend. Unless I sold one of my paintings, the car was probably the next—make that *last*—of my personal possessions that would have to be sold to pay for that storage unit. And then what?

"Is your family really like that? Will they eat me alive?"

"Not at all. They'll kill you first. Then eat you." We descended the hill, and then we turned right onto Society Row. My parents lived in one of the big Victorian mansions originally built by the most prosperous and prominent citizens of the town a hundred or so years ago. Theirs wasn't the grandest, not compared to Winterford or to the Layton place or Swansdown, but it held its own. And they were right proud of it.

Too soon for either of us, I suspected, we were parked in front of the large, two-story mansion. Its windows each held a holiday candelabra, with ironic glowing and welcoming gleams.

Or, *was* it ironic? How would they receive me? Us?

"Let's go." Hazel reached across and placed a light touch on my forearm. "You belong to them. They miss you. No matter what."

Maybe, maybe not. But we went inside anyway and were slammed with a wall of noisy conversation, kid-yelps, holiday tunes blaring through the stereo speakers, and another wall of the smell of cooking turkey and stuffing. My stomach growled, and Hazel looked up at me, slipping her hand into mine—her right hand, the one that needed the most security.

The one everyone will try to shake when they meet her.

Oh, why had I invited her to this potential minefield? Everything about it could explode her life in an instant. How selfish was I to even dream of putting her through it?

"Isaac?" My mother's voice shrilled through the air, and all other noise except the stereo came to a thundering silence. Then, someone shut off the music, and the effect was complete. "You came?"

"Hi, Mom." I waited, and she approached.

Mom stood in front of me, while everyone else in the room held their collective breath. For an eternal moment, she appraised me, searching me from head to toe, pausing on my face, her eyes darting all over as if assessing whether it was really me or some cruel impersonation.

"It's really me, in case you're wondering."

"I can see that." No hug of welcome. No thawing of the glacier. "And who's this?"

Why not just drop the bomb immediately? I gave her full name. "This is Hazel Hollings. You remember her."

Hazel nodded to Mom. Blessedly, Mom did not offer to shake Hazel's hand. Rude, but much less awkward for Hazel. Probably. "It's nice to meet you, Mrs. Ivey. Ike is such a good man. Thanks for raising him so well."

For a split second, a look of confusion flitted across Mom's face, a quick triple-blink, as if she were a machine resetting. But then she took up the usual mask again. "I see you've maintained your relations with *that* family." She frowned. "Wasn't one generation of Hollingses in your life enough?"

85

"No, Mom. And Hazel is great. You know what she has done with her life, how well she has represented Massey Falls to the whole world."

Before Mom could respond, Mom's sister Una Mae strode up and threw her arms around Hazel. "Why, if it isn't our child prodigy. Everyone! Hazel Hollings is here with us—direct from the highest echelons of the arts world in Reedsville. Isn't it lovely? People, let's get her a plate of turkey and stuffing. Dora"—that was my mom—"ask Hazel what her favorite pie is, and I'll be a monkey's uncle if she doesn't say *hazelnut*. Bring her a piece of hazelnut pie, Felix."

My weird cousin Felix jumped at his mother's command, and in no time, Hazel and I were safely settled and being served large china plates of holiday foods.

Aunt Una Mae leaned over and hissed into my ear. "That's how we in the Ladies' Auxiliary handle the awkward situations, and why your mom has not yet qualified for membership."

I gave the tiniest nod of acknowledgment, just as Aunt Una Mae would want.

With my aunt's powerful cloak of indemnity, we made it through dinner and carols and the nativity play unscathed. The only thing coming our way was a series of polite, if strained, smiles and a few genuine nods of remembrance. At least some of my cousins seemed glad. A few mouthed their *good to see yous* and *hey, buddies*. It wasn't exactly the roaring welcome of hail the conquering hero, but I hadn't been thrown out on my rear end, either.

Maybe that was thanks to Hazel's close clinging to my side. Until she left to use the restroom, and I was standing alone. Up walked my mother.

"Hazel Hollings? Of all people. How could you?"

"She's great, Mom. You have to see that."

"Oh, I see it. I see that she's worlds too good for you. You couldn't even keep hold of the likes of Topanga Tycho, the Hazel wannabe. She dropped you like a spiky pine cone, and if Hazel were smart, she wouldn't touch you with hot tongs. Does she know the truth about you? About your past with Topanga, about the real reasons that you're not a good risk, son, for any thinking woman."

"Thanks, Mom. I love your confidence in me. It's contagious." And as deadly as an engineered virus. She wasn't wrong about any of it, but hearing so didn't feel great either. "I might not be as much of a red flag as you think, Mom. Trust me." It took all my restraint not to brag about the ceiling art commission, or the fact that Trey Tycho would be seeing it soon, and that Ms. Eileen obviously believed in my talent and skills enough to arrange for the art magnate to view it as an eyewitness.

No, Mom hadn't earned that information. Someday, maybe, she would understand. It killed me a little to be so easily dismissed, but someday, if I proved myself, she might forgive me for not becoming her narrow definition of success. It stunk to admit that my own mother needed cold, hard numbers to accept that her son was worthy, but, after all, she'd been married to my dad for over thirty years, and he'd obviously rubbed off on her over time.

Instead, I changed the topic. "What do you hear from Calvin?"

Calvin Turner was my *other* cousin, and her favorite nephew. He lived in Reedsville, working as an advertising consultant to big companies like SolutionX. She liked holding me up to his standard— but what she didn't know was that Calvin had run through a string of girlfriends so long he could've knitted an army's worth of sweaters with it.

"He's doing *so* well." Mom gushed for a minute about Calvin's successes. "His mom calls weekly to tell me about Calvin's latest girlfriend."

Was that a success? In Mom's book, it probably was. In mine, not so much.

That said, Calvin always showed up for events, supported family members, and kept the laughs coming. I liked the guy—even though he served as my social foil.

Before I could be held up as a pale comparison to Calvin for much longer, Mom got called away by Felix, her least-favorite nephew. Whew.

Hazel came back, bringing me a mug of steaming spiced apple cider. We sat together on a loveseat, and sipped. I needed to tell her about the medical school debt, but we were at a party, and there was enough tension in the air as it was.

Speaking of tension … Ah, now it was Dad's turn.

"So, you're back." My dad loomed over our loveseat, gripping a clear glass of eggnog and swaying. It was not his first serving of the hard stuff. He'd been to the pitcher full of *adult* eggnog a few times, and that was only while I was noticing. His eyes were a little bloodshot, and his speech showed that he'd imbibed. His *s* in *so* had come out *sho*. *Sho, you're back.*

"Hi, Dad. Have you met Hazel? She's home for the holidays." We both stood up to greet him.

Dad sniffed. "Is she going to play the organ for us? Tell her to go play it." He was not a good drinker.

"We don't have an organ, Dad." Thank goodness. At least I had that defense.

Speaking of defense, Hazel came to mine—albeit in the worst way possible. "Hello, Mr. Ivey. I'm pleased to meet you. Ike is amazing. He's creating a great piece of artwork, you know."

Zing. My dad's anger-switch flipped to *on,* and his whole head and face purpled. "Art!" he blasted. "Blast art! My son is a doctor!"

"Maybe not officially, but he's definitely a healer, sir." Hazel couldn't have stood closer to my side if we'd been Siamese twins. "I was injured a few months ago, and with Ike's help, I'm getting through it."

For whatever reason, this calmed Dad, and he only stood there frowning. After a couple of seconds, he turned toward me. "You got your MD and didn't tell me? You're saying your Loser Choice days are over? They were only my bad dream?" He opened his mouth to say more, but Hazel asserted herself again.

"Everyone's invited to the Falls View Chapel on Christmas Eve for the candle-lighting service. It's going to be stellar this year, one for the ages. I hope you'll come."

Aunt Una Mae, a few paces away, seemed to have spotted the situation. Her eyes bugged out, and she sprang into action. In two steps, she was at Dad's side, turning him toward the buffet. "We're all planning on it, dears. Dora and Dean here have it engraved on their social calendar." She spoke louder, and directly into Dad's ear, "Isn't that right, Deano?"

I collapsed back onto the couch, and Hazel cuddled up next to me.

"That went well," she said, and then busted out a laugh. It was the first time I'd heard that laugh in ages. It began with a low rumble and ended with a high giggle. So cute. "Sorry for picking the wrong thing to brag about. But, hey. Your aunt will get them to the unveiling of your art. She's a force of nature."

"Una Mae makes the hurricane that is Ms. Eileen look like a spring zephyr." I grimaced.

"Sorry about my dad."

"Don't give it another thought. If anyone gets it, I do."

That was likely true. Oh, brother. "Well, if it's any consolation, I've never touched the stuff and never will."

"Same." She crossed her heart, and then poked her index finger toward her eye.

"Seriously, no needles in the eye, though. That's too freaky." I pulled her beside me and we pushed on through the social extravaganza that was the Ivey family Christmas party.

We finished the evening without further incident from Mom or Dad, but the whole thing left me rocked to my foundations. *Mom and Dad are coming to see my art. They'll get a big shock when they do.*

As we were leaving, Hazel asked me to help her with her seatbelt, as I'd been delighted to do lately.

"Gladly," I said, and gave her a light kiss as I reached across to fasten it. "Any other requests?"

"Just to see the art you have in storage, the ones I have bragged about incessantly to strangers, sight-unseen."

It was only fair. I did owe it to her. "It's a few minutes' drive. You're all right going into a dark storage facility at night with a known kissaholic?"

"Yes, please," she said, and I stepped on the gas. This might be a good, private time to give her the Christmas present I'd had copied and spiral-bound for her. No one would bother us while we were viewing the paintings. When we parked in the side lot at Clint's Climate-Controlled Cubbies, I grabbed my satchel, which had both the key to the unit and the gift for Hazel. For the first time tonight, I zinged with anticipation instead of dread. What she'd think of the paintings paled in comparison to the question of what she'd think of my attempt to please her with this gift.

I placed the key in the lock and turned it, waiting for the multiple clicks. With a loud creak, the door swung open and revealed the purposely dark room. The gauge showed the temperature was a perfect sixty-eight degrees, with the humidity still in the ideal range between forty-five and fifty percent. Ah, at least my money was not being wasted. My paintings were preserved as much as humanly possible. Much better than if they'd been in Mom and Dad's garage or attic, actually, so in a way, I ought to thank them for their rejection of my request to keep them there.

I turned on the light.

"Are they lying in these cubbies?" Hazel stepped toward the shelving that I'd brought in for storing them flat. "Which one should I see first?"

Over the next hour, I pulled out all sixty-three of my designs, one by one. She insisted on seeing them all—from bighorn sheep atop a rocky bluff, to the lone blossom of a saguaro cactus in the Sonora after a violent rain, to the deep grays and blues of moonlight shining on longhorn cattle with the buttes of Monument Valley in the background.

Upon viewing each new piece, she pointed out details she admired and symbolism I was impressed she had spotted. She eloquently expressed the overall emotion the painting as a whole elicited in her. If something didn't strike her as quite right, she pointed that out, too. Maybe someone else's similar comment would have brought up my hackles, but when it came from Hazel, all I could think as a reaction was how much I wanted to make the next version better.

More perfect. For her.

Hazel Hollings was the perfect person to show all my artwork to. I couldn't have imagined a more ideal audience or critic. I couldn't have fantasized, even as a younger man, that Hazel herself was as incredible as the real-life version of her turned out to be.

"You're my dream girl," I said, gushing in the thrill of the moment.

"Because you only think of me as a dream and not a reality?" she asked, with a surprising wariness in her tone.

"Because I dream of you night and day." It was time. I reached for the satchel leaning against the wall and pulled out the gift. "I didn't wrap it."

"Men don't really wrap stuff, in my experience," she said as she accepted it with her left hand and steadied it with her right.

Oh, and look at that! Three fingers of her right hand had extended a little. They weren't as gripped into a fist as before, and the skin of the back of her hand was less red. I could have grabbed and kissed it for joy, but she started opening the book I'd almost decided not to give her.

"Is this ...?" She raised her head and met my eyes. "You made this for me?"

"Do you think you can play from it?"

"Ike! It's all the songs from the annual candle-lighting service, but arranged for left hand. Where did you get it?"

"There's a pianist by the name of Snell. He has quite a story." I summarized it quickly, just sharing that Dr. Snell, too, had suffered a right-hand injury. "For years, he reverted to only selecting music for piano instruction books and to publishing or composing for others, even though he couldn't play the songs he'd written. But then, one day, he realized how much he missed playing the songs himself, so he took up the challenge and arranged his favorite music for left-hand only. He has a whole library of songs for pianists like himself."

"And like me," Hazel said, her voice barely a whisper. "Oh, Ike. Thank you. *Thank you.*" Tears welled and then spilled, almost splashed, down her cheeks. She threw her arms around me and kissed me like I'd done the best thing for her in the whole world. "I'm grateful beyond measure. If I'd known this was an option, I wouldn't have let Topanga highjack my spot playing for the candle-lighting service."

I pulled away. "Topanga? She's playing for the service in your place?"

Chapter 13

Hazel

I lay in my bed and stared at the ceiling, holding my aching fingers to my lips, and recounting the evening's disaster—like the chaos of a Black Friday-crazed mob storming through my soul.

At least I had Christmas with Aunt Gretchen to look forward to. Just a quiet, pleasant gift-exchange, a few carols, Chinese food, and then we'd sink into the beanbags and watch all our favorite holiday films.

Simple.

The Christmas I'd been missing all these years since Dad died.

It was so great to have that to look forward to, so great that no matter what, I wouldn't be alone this year.

Speaking of gifts, that sheet music! I couldn't wait to play it. If the clock hadn't already struck way-past-bedtime, I'd be up in the chapel plucking out all the notes already. That had to be the sweetest, most thoughtful thing anyone had ever done for me, period.

On the flip side, Ike's reaction to Topanga's name during that conversation with me at the storage unit had seriously flattened my tires. Conflicted storms had thundered through his countenance. Zero doubt—he still harbored feelings for her. Whether they were good or bad, there was no clear clue, and I could ask him, but why? Why bring up my rival and remind him of his old feelings for her? It had been bad enough that I'd merely dropped her name in connection with the candle-lighting service—and look what it'd done to him. Holy nuclear reaction, Batman.

Sure, he'd quickly recovered. It confirmed what I'd heard him say to his mom during their family party. Well, what I thought I'd heard. They were definitely talking about his relationship with Topanga. If that were fully wrapped up, would his mom be mentioning it?

Not that his mom seemed like the most sensitive person. She might be the type to bring up past failed relationships, just out of spite. Argh, how could he stand it? The dad, too. Well, I could empathize there, thanks to my dad's own slow decline, which had appeared to be alcoholism from all external evidence. But no doctor ever knew how to help him, nor could he have afforded one that could diagnose him.

I had to admit it relieved me to hear that Ike would never take a drop of it, regardless.

Man, he had me on the whiplash machine. One second, I was all in, and the next, I wanted to run away and hide. Oh, but then I'd recall the way his kisses turned me into apple butter—homemade by that multi-talented man—and I was all done for again. Complete gone-zo.

If he was still into Topanga on the side, that wasn't great.

The front door banged open and then shut. "Hola, sweetie. You home?"

"Hey." I rolled out of bed and padded into the main room to hug Aunt Gretchen, who was rolling two large suitcases out of her bedroom and perched them next to the front door. "Why do you have your bags packed?"

"You know me! I have to be ready to leave at any moment."

Right. That was true. I could exhale. "You're still planning to be here on Christmas, though, right?"

"Sure, sure." She was looking at her phone screen, swiping and swiping. "Sorry, this will only take a second. Then I want to hear all about the shark tank you just endured."

It was over an hour later, and Aunt Gretchen was still on the line with someone in Sapporo, so I let myself drift off to another topic. The real shark—Trey Tycho.

"Whatcha thinking about that makes your brow get so wrinkled?" Gretchen ran a finger across my forehead to smooth it as she entered the room. "You keep a-worrying, and it'll stay like that."

"It's the Trey Tycho wrinkle, and it's not just on my forehead, it's imprinted on my soul." I told her about my worries while we sat on the couch and ate pistachios until the shell pile could've filled Santa's whole sleigh. "So, if you were me, what would you do? Would you endanger the man you love, by association?"

"It's love we're calling it now, is it?" She belted a single laugh. "Oh, honey. I've seen proof of that for weeks now. Longer, actually. Since you were a goofy kid and chose your favorite candy based on the guy's name. Now, back to your dilemma. What would I do? I'd absolutely dump him."

"Dump him!" My spine went straight as a rod, and I knocked about a quart of those little wooden shells onto the carpet. "Why?"

"Because I'd tell myself it was the only way to protect him from guilt by association. Trey Tycho, if he hated me, wouldn't touch my boyfriend with hot tongs."

There was that horrid phrase again. What did it even mean?

"So you're saying I should tell him it's over?"

"No, sweetie! Of course not! You asked what *I* would do. And you know that *I always* make the wrong choice when it comes to men. That's why I'm fifty and still single. But I've seen the world, and that's some consolation."

Uh-huh. So what exactly was she telling me to do?

And should I listen to Gretchen anyway?

If I'd thought I couldn't sleep earlier, now that I'd heard that harsh reality, I suffered ten times the insomnia attack. What was I going to do to help Ike the way he'd helped me?

Aunt Gretchen had to be right.

With my painfully slow method of using my left forefinger, I typed up a text.

It's going to be best if we don't see each other anymore. I hope you can understand someday. Promise, it's not you, it's me. A hundred percent.

However, again, as the world's crawlingest coward, I shut off my phone and didn't send it.

Chapter 14

Ike

The ceiling painting progressed like a house afire, now that Hazel could play so many songs. She spent all our working time at the organ bench brushing up on her skills and improving hour by hour. She even seemed so absorbed by it that she didn't come out to lunch with me when I asked. After a few days, I was getting serious Hazel withdrawals.

But I understood. She was making a sacrifice—on my behalf. She wanted me to finish, and she'd postpone even meals together to keep my focus riveted on the task. And good thing, too, since each passing day brought us closer to the proverbial monster at the end of the book—Christmas Eve and the candle-lighting service.

Luckily, I didn't have to stop painting when Topanga came into the chapel to preempt Hazel's practicing. I'd always put on my headphones and ignore her. She seemed just as content to ignore me, a major Christmas miracle.

The days passed too quickly, and all of a sudden, I was adding my signature to one corner of the completed painting. The scaffolding had obscured portions of it from the view of anyone passing through, including Hazel and Topanga. Only I had seen the expanse, and from too close a proximity to get the full effect.

On Christmas Eve morning, the scaffolding-rental removal crew showed up and disassembled the whole thing. Instantly, the church women's society descended, shooing me out of the room so they could do their magic of sprucing up the area for the candle lighting.

Hours later, I came back to check, since I hadn't even had time to examine the effect of what I'd created. No one was around, so I lay down flat on my back on one of the now-bunting-laden central pews. Thirty-feet above, the story I'd created stretched across the expanse of the central panel of the ceiling.

From end to end—the morning star to the daystar, the night sky and the desert and the parable's symbolic motif … *it had worked!* I might have choked up a little bit and fought my way through a sniffle. Oh, my goodness, who'd turned me into Hazel Hollings, because now it was my eyes flooding and threatening a downpour. I couldn't catch a breath.

"Hazel," I whispered almost silently into the empty room. "We did it."

If only she were here in the room right this moment to experience it with me. I'd barely heard from her, as she'd been respecting my intense focus, but now, all that was passed, and I wanted to take her in my arms, to spend every waking second showing her how much I—

"It's amazing." Footfalls filled the cavernous room.

Some woman, *not Hazel,* was there in the chapel, and I sat up fast, swiping at my cheeks in case of stray moisture. When I turned, there stood Topanga.

Ugh, she was the last person I'd wanted to experience the painting first. "Let's go talk in the foyer," I said, trying to get her away from the painting.

"Why? So your so-called girlfriend gets to gush with you over the finished product?" She complained, but I steered her into the hallway at the back of the chapel. "I'm here to warn you, Ike. You're going to need to impress my dad tonight. The only way to do that is to make up with me."

"Make up with you? You're the one who dumped me, Topanga."

"All the same, I'm not uninterested in your success. In fact, it would be a serious boost to my reputation if you turn out to be the boy

98

wonder of the local art scene. I'd love to be able to be the one to say I discovered you first and steered you to Daddy. Why do you think the one and only Trey Tycho is coming to podunk little Massey Falls on a night as important in the arts world as Christmas Eve? Hmm?"

She'd done that? I didn't believe a word of it. "Ms. Eileen invited him."

"At my behest. You don't see Ms. Eileen shunning me, do you? She even replaced your so-called child prodigy at the organ with me. You can see she has a clear preference, and it's not just for me. It's for you too. We are her chosen pairing. Don't you get it?" She slinked her long legs and willowy body toward me and snaked her palm up my arm, paused to stroke the side of my neck and then came up on tiptoe to whisper in my ear. "The two of us could be explosive."

I jumped out of her reach. "Topanga, this isn't a good idea."

"The show starts in two hours. Spend those hours with me, Isaac." She'd attached herself to me again. I brushed her off, but she returned. "You'll see. I'm your bridge to Daddy. And Daddy is your bridge to your career's future. Don't you know Daddy is the one who fired Hazel? After she ruined his million-dollar concert? He's suing her for damages."

The ringing got louder the more she spoke, and the more punches landed in my gut.

"Your father is the one who produced the global choir festival?" My voice came from far away. "It was his concert?" I repeated lamely.

"Who else?" Topanga gave that laugh of hers, the one that made the stained glass rattle in its leaded frames. "He's the king- and queen-maker of the arts world in our realm, Isaac. With her talent, Hazel was nearly crowned, but then she betrayed him by ruining all the things he'd set up on her behalf. I can't say I lost much sleep over it. Mom was forever comparing me to her. Hazel this, Hazel that. *Why don't you practice as much as Hazel? Your dad will never see your talent until you're like Hazel.* When, seriously, I was putting in at least as many hours as that daughter of a drunken landscape worker." Topanga huffed.

99

"What did she have that I didn't have? Especially after I convinced *you* to come over to the box seats of life instead of the standing room only cheap seats. So, Isaac. Will you have me as your bridge to success?"

My phone pinged a text. I reached for it. Oh, hallelujah. It was from Hazel.

It's going to be best if we don't see each other anymore. I hope you can understand someday. Promise, it's not you, it's me. A hundred percent.

A loud buzzing rose all around me. Topanga was speaking through a long, tinny tunnel.

The doors for the event opened, and guests started streaming in, including Ms. Eileen, and my conversation with Topanga ended like a book snapping shut. Ms. Eileen whisked me into the chapel, where she praised the ceiling and bragged to her friends that she'd discovered me.

My ears rang even louder. Tinnitus had struck hard. The phone with Hazel's text was still glued to the center of my palm. I couldn't bring myself to look at it again to verify what I'd seen. With some difficulty, I answered questions from Ms. Eileen's friends, until the chapel filled with a booming excess of pipes from the organ where Topanga sat and played "Silent Night" with a grandiose exuberance.

If it'd been Hazel there, and if she hadn't just told me we were through, I would have resonated with the beauty and sacredness she would have brought to that hymn with every fiber of my soul. My art was acceptable to Ms. Eileen, even loved. And my parents were coming, and Ms. Eileen would surely gush all over them for it, which might even heal some bitter waters.

But without Hazel, none of it felt triumphant. None of it felt real. None of it even mattered.

Hazel, why? Why not us? Why now?

Chapter 15

Hazel

"Seriously?" I wanted to shake Aunt Gretchen. "You're leaving *now?*" It was Christmas Eve, and the candle-lighting service was set to begin in half an hour. "What about our plans?"

"Honey, there's a storm in the forecast. If they shut the airports after midnight, I won't catch a flight to Peru until next week. Or longer. The company needs me there to oversee the distribution of all those toys I collected. They're already crated and on their way to the airport. I'm hamstrung here. You do know I love you, right? And that I'd never choose other people over *us* if there were any way around it."

That was exactly what she was doing, though. Couldn't she see that?

"You're going to be great tonight, though. I can't wait for you to show the world that your left-hand playing is as strong as any two-handed organist in the world. You're amazing." She pressed her palms against the sides of my face and kissed the top of my head with a loud *mmwah!* It didn't comfort me. It wasn't enough. She had no idea that it would be Topanga playing the organ tonight, and not me.

Sentiment wasn't enough. Presence was what mattered.

In my agitation, I next made a fatal error. I left the apartment and headed upstairs to the chapel to look for Ike and see whether he'd come back to the chapel so we could look at the ceiling together. But something stopped me. A voice.

And from the midpoint of the stairs, a scene unfolded before me, and I shrank back into the shadows begging for what I thought was happening to *not* be happening.

And yet, there stood Ike and Topanga together in the foyer in a heated discussion, one not intended for my ears. But did I retreat? Not soon enough. Really, I should have just turned my sorry little self around and returned to Aunt Gretchen and helped her finish packing. Instead, I tuned my ears to someone else's conversation. Topanga was speaking.

You're going to need to impress my dad tonight. The only way to do that is to make up with me.

It took everything in me to steady my breath. What was she saying? Did she mean it? It couldn't be true—she wasn't begging for them to be together, was she? And yet, I'd heard what I'd heard. I missed a few things, but when I was able to tune in again, Topanga was speaking again.

I discovered you first and steered you to Daddy. Why do you think the one and only Trey Tycho is coming to podunk little Massey Falls on a night as important in the arts world as Christmas Eve? Hmm?

But—but, my dad discovered Ike first! My feet lurched, almost forcing me up the stairs to rebut her claim, but the slithering coward in me prevailed, and the smallest part of my soul must have taken the wheel because I kept on swimming in the sludge of the eavesdropper.

What came next gave me an earful toxic enough to make me do something rash.

You'll see, Ike. I'm your bridge to Daddy. And Daddy is your bridge to your career's future. Don't you know Daddy is the one who fired Hazel? After she ruined his million-dollar concert?

The horrible fact was real: Topanga had spilled the truth to Ike that I should have told him weeks ago.

My innards crushed like a bag of potato chips on the floor of a rock concert. I sped down the stairs and sent that text that had lurked in my phone unsent, waiting to detonate a relationship that had been my dream for a decade. Maybe for all eternity.

But it was over. And done with.

I hiccupped. I couldn't help it. But if Topanga wanted him and could help him, which she obviously could while I couldn't, what choice was I left with if I truly loved him? She hadn't been wrong, she was absolutely his best bridge to success. Who was I to argue with that? I was a bridge breaker, and she was a bridge builder for him, the exact person he needed to reach the success he desired. I was nothing but a hindrance.

My tears really did come then. I strode through the apartment and straight into my room. Aunt Gretchen just gave me a wave while she talked on her phone.

Some Christmas Eve.

Chapter 16

Ike

I paced the hall outside the chapel doors. Evan emerged from the big room where the candle-lighting service was about to begin, holding a fussing niece in his arms.

"Ike, my friend, your ceiling is a hit." Evan held up a palm for a high five, but my arms felt pinned to my sides. "What's wrong, buddy? You just made a beautiful room absolutely spectacular, and everyone is loving it. I have to say, I wouldn't have guessed that a Western scene could be so religious. You have to think about it to get the meaning, but it works. It really works."

Topanga's organ music blasted louder as another patron exited and headed toward the restrooms, and then it quieted again.

"Thanks, Evan. Who's this?"

He talked about his niece for a moment, and then he stabbed a finger into my collarbone. "What's the matter? Nerves? You think Trey Tycho is in there deconstructing every brush stroke of your work? It's *dim*. They're lighting *candles*. He's admiring his daughter's musicality. You're not on trial here. Say, why isn't Hazel Hollings the one playing?"

"She"—I nearly told her secret—"wasn't feeling up to it." That was true.

"Then if she's sick you should be hovering over that gorgeous musician with chicken soup, shouldn't you? And reading her fairy tales. And bringing her vases with single rosebuds. What's wrong with you?

Get downstairs!"

My shoulders fell, and my innards collapsed, like a blown-out tire on the freeway. "I would, but she broke up with me."

Evan's eyes bugged out. "Why did she do that?"

"I have no idea. But I guess I deserve it, because I didn't defend her when I should have."

"Someone attacked Hazel? She's so sweet. Who could be mean to her? That's absurd."

"Exactly." But *Trey Tycho* had been a beast to her, and when faced with the choice between my career and standing up for Hazel, I'd blown it. And for some reason, as if she'd been clairvoyant and read the sorry weakness of my least manly thoughts in the very moment they occurred, she'd cut me off.

Although, she would have probably seen it as setting me free. Liberating me from the cords that tied me down to her. And for that split second when Topanga had offered me what had seemed like the world, I'd hesitated. I'd reached for the brass ring, mentally, and that was the precise timing of the breakup text from Hazel.

What was I supposed to think or do?

"I gotta get back in there." The baby in Evan's arms had fallen asleep. "Cheryl won't love being stuck with two toddlers alone in the meeting. But Ike, my friend, I think you'll figure out what's right and do it. You always do."

"I do?"

"Sure. You cut loose from medical school the second you realized it was taking you down a road that wasn't for you. I've always admired that. It took courage to stand up to your parents—who don't exactly deserve *Parents of the Century* awards for their poor treatment of you after that gutsy choice, by the way—and you walked away from Topanga Tycho when she revealed her real character, and you never looked back."

Didn't I? "She's the one who dumped me when I made the Loser Choice."

"Stop calling it that. You've created a world-class artwork in that room." He chin-jutted toward the chapel, so as not to move his arm from under the sleeping child. "Trey Tycho is going to see that, whether or not you're dating his daughter. That, or he's virtually blind. And a bit of a jerk. And you wouldn't want to deal with him anyway. Not with all the other art experts who'll be wanting to throw the big bucks at you. Now, I gotta go. That pep talk was free, but once I pass the bar, I'll be charging by the hour."

Evan slid back into the meeting, and I found a bench to wait on where I could think.

What he'd said might have some truth to it, but the fact remained that Hazel had dropped me. I sent her another text. It went unreceived. I dialed her number. It didn't go through. She either had her phone off or she'd blocked me. I could walk down the stairs and beg her forgiveness. Duh, why hadn't I thought of that? I headed across the hallway to the staircase that led to the basement apartment, but I met a taxi driver. "I'm here to pick up bags for a Ms. Hollings?"

"Down the stairs." I pointed, my soul reeling.

She was leaving? On Christmas Eve?

I stumbled backward, just as the doors to the chapel burst open, and what seemed like the entire congregation exited the room. Several of them recognized me right away, and in a moment, I was surrounded by newly minted fans of Ike Ivey's cowboy ceiling art.

"Ike, what you created in there is marvelous!"

"It's exactly the unique touch that Falls View Chapel has needed for ages."

"If they would've just turned on the lights during the candle service we could've admired it better."

"Cowboys don't belong in church," grumbled one man, and that comment was quickly challenged by a woman who said, "That's rich, coming from a crusty old son-of-a-rancher like you, Wyatt."

The sea of art appreciators parted, however, for my parents. First, my mom walked up, wearing a frown. "We weren't expecting that."

"No, we weren't." Dad wore a similar frown, plus he'd folded his arms over his chest. "You aren't as amateurish as I would have expected."

"Amateurish!" A booming voice split the air. "Ike, my boy. Come and let's discuss your future."

Trey Tycho.

This moment constituted my biggest decision in life. Far bigger than whether to drop out of medical school.

"Yes, sir. I think we probably do have some things to discuss."

Chapter 17

Hazel

Aunt Gretchen apologized for the tenth time and then left to catch her waiting taxi to the airport. The apartment where I'd grown up more or less echoed with hollow emptiness. Footfalls of the exiting crowd clunked faintly against the ceiling. I'd missed Ike's unveiling. I'd missed the candle-lighting service, my favorite event of the year. Falls View Chapel didn't hold midnight services, and soon even the upstairs would be empty.

I'd be alone any minute now.

Truly alone.

From upstairs, the strains of "Silent Night" had signaled the beginning of the candle-lighting service. I'd memorized that hymn years ago, and I'd been working on it with left-hand-only. I knew exactly where my fingers and feet would have been placed on the keys and pedals.

I sat at the table and went through the motions, eyes closed. "Silent night," I air-played the chord and the melody, picturing the light of the first candle flickering to life in the grip of whoever was chosen. "All is calm." The first person tilted the flame to light the candle of the person beside him. "Sleep in heavenly peace." By the third verse, everyone in the room would be holding a light, and the room would be warm in a collective, unifying radiance.

And I had missed it. Not just playing the hymn. Not seeing or feeling that glowing connection with all the people of Falls View

Chapel. But I had missed experiencing it with Ike.

Cue the pity-party buffet.

Buffet? Yeah. Food. I needed food.

In the cupboard sat a lone cellophane-covered bag of microwave popcorn. I unwrapped it and stuck it in the microwave, and stood there staring at the wall. Before I knew it, the darn thing had overcooked, smoke and everything. Great, now my whole apartment smelled like burnt popcorn.

Festive.

Very festive.

And possibly a little symbolic, since I'd burned my bridges with pretty much everyone in my life now. Mainly Ike. He was the only one my heart could focus on, anyway. There was a crater-sized hole in my soul without him.

I pinched the edges of the hot popcorn bag and took it up the stairs and outside to the dumpster, freezing all the way without my coat. Back downstairs, I turned on every possible fan, but the smell persisted. I curled up on the couch and got yet another tissue. One box-worth already lay in damp wads in the trash can beside the end table, and this one was nearly out. Curse my easy-crier curse. At this rate, I'd dehydrate myself by midnight, before Santa could even arrive.

I curled up on the sofa with a too-short throw blanket that didn't cover my feet and eventually fell asleep.

A knock came at the door. It was still dark out, though the Christmas tree's lights glowed, and I sat up groggily. The glowing digital clock read six fifteen. Christmas morning, who could be at the door?

Ike? Please let it be Ike, come to talk me out of my choice.

I reached for my hair—was it a mess? I'd put it in a lumpy ponytail. I patted beneath my eyes. Whoa, what puffy bags! It's what I got for crying half the night. Never mind. I raced over and threw it open, looking upward for his face, only to be greeted by Ms. Eileen, who was my own height instead.

109

"Oh, Hazel! You're up. Thank goodness." She moved past me into the apartment. "What happened in here? Are you burning popcorn on purpose? Where is Gretchen's map with all the pins in it from the places she's traveled? Listen, we've had a disaster for this morning. Can you play the organ for matins? Topanga Tycho has other things to do."

Yeah, probably making out with Ike as they plan their shining future together.

"What songs are you hoping for?"

"Oh, anything you want. Just give me a list."

My mind shot to the booklet Ike had made for me. It not only contained the hymns for last night's candle-lighting service, but a few that would be appropriate for the congregation to sing during matins or any other celebration. "What about 'Hark, the Herald Angels Sing' or 'Joy to the World?' And is it okay if they're an octave lower, just to spice things up?" And just so I could actually play them? "I'm working on some new techniques, and I'd like to give them a dry run today."

"Anything you like. You're the one doing me a huge favor."

I gave a whole list to her, and she jotted them down. "Now, Hazel. You didn't show yourself at the candle-lighting service last night. Why not? There were several people looking for you, from far and wide. Even someone from Mendon, a good-looking young man I hadn't met before. And what a shame for you not to see the debut of Isaac's artwork when you'd been working with him so closely all this time. What about friendship and loyalty?"

Yeah, what about them? Ike had dumped ours by hitching his wagon to Topanga's star at the first offering. I'd let him go, but only out of loyalty. "We're still friends." Forever. I'd think of my friendship and connection to him as the most important of my life. "No matter what. And I'm really happy for his major success. Trey Tycho couldn't have helped being struck by the majesty of Ike's piece. It was original and true to his style. I'm wishing them the best in their future business partnership."

Ms. Eileen's eyes practically bugged out. "Business partnership!"

110

She shook from head to toe.

"Sure."

Ms. Eileen frowned, but she didn't elaborate.

Hadn't that business arrangement gone forward? It must have—unless she was frowning because of a familial partnership that loomed. Had the inevitable marriage of Ike to Topanga already been discussed? After all, they'd dated steadily for a long time back in the day. One reconciliation might be all it had taken for them to leapfrog forward. Especially after all Topanga suggested about being his bridge and about their complete symbiotic need for each other.

"I'll be happy to play for matins at ten, but I need to get ready and to practice a little. I'll see you there." I somewhat herded her toward the door.

"Hazel—" Ms. Eileen turned toward me. "Never mind. I'll just see you at matins. Thank you for playing."

Never mind what? I ached to ask her, but my pride didn't let me.

Before leaving, she glanced at my right hand, which I'd allowed to slip out. "Oh, dear. Your hand is so red. Did you burn it when you smoked up the apartment with that popcorn fire?"

Instantly, I retracted it into the sleeve. "It's all right. See you later."

"Hazel, darling, I'm your second mom. Tell me."

No, Aunt Gretchen was my second mom. And she left me alone. On Christmas.

"If you don't hustle, you'll miss your grandkids waking up and seeing the tree and the presents, won't you?" I helped her out the door and shut it behind her.

Then, I showered and dressed and went upstairs to practice the songs we'd discussed for matins. However, even my left hand was having trouble this morning. It was insanely cold in the chapel, and my belly kept trembling, and my fingers creaked with some kind of arthritic lassitude. They ached.

Or maybe that was my heart.

When the sun finally came up around eight, splashing light through the windows, the room was illuminated, and I took a moment to rest my fingers and feet—and to look up at Ike's creation on the ceiling. Oh, how glorious! Every inch of the massive work brought feeling and insight. I climbed off the bench and circled the area beneath it, weaving between the pews to see the thing from different angles. Bits of it had always been obscured while he was working on it, due to the massive view-blocking scaffold and platform, so I'd never experienced the full effect before. It sluiced through me like a flood of truth and light.

My tears agreed. For once, I didn't curse them. In fact, I couldn't help laughing my way through them. They were spot-on in their timing for once.

"It's brilliant," I whispered. "You did it, Ike."

Footfalls sounded. The chapel began to fill for matins, and I returned to the bench of the organ and played a few pedal-only etudes that I'd memorized for practice years ago as a student. They didn't sound like Christmas, but they did sound musical. And the organ always sounded like Christmas, right? Sort of—unless someone played it poorly, like I was doing now.

Oh, and look at who'd just walked in and sat on the front row. Topanga herself. I nearly slipped off the bench into a coma. Again.

The notes barely connected anymore, with her eyeing me and frowning like that. I'd better quit glancing her direction. Not only did both my hands hurt, but my toes did too. Why was she here? Why was she alone? Shouldn't she be with Ike, kissing? Enjoying Christmas morning with his family who adored her?

And where was he? Oh! Maybe he'd gone off to paint her a picture, something private, just for her. A nude, maybe. Good heavens! What was I even thinking?

I flubbed a bunch of notes, the chord coming off like a goose's honk. A goose that should've been cooked for Christmas dinner instead.

Hey, self! You're ruining matins. For everyone. Stop thinking about nude art in the chapel on Christmas morning. What was wrong with me?

Everything.

Luckily, the service began, so I could quit wrecking the prelude. I muddled through the opening hymn with not a few mistakes. The congregation didn't seem to notice, but the song leader gave me a puzzled look when she went to sit down. She was new since I'd lived here. Maybe her expectations were low? And yet still unmet?

During the interim between song disasters, while the sermon began, my right hand hurt more than it ever had, and the left obviously wasn't cooperating much better than during my warm-up before the service.

The sermon was blessedly short, and it included a retelling of the Christmas story and a lesson about keeping Christmas in our hearts all year long.

No problem here. For me, this Christmas meant cold and loneliness and burnt popcorn and burnt bridges. Easy to replicate.

We began the closing hymn, and my playing got steadily worse. The song leader turned and shot me a very concerned look, as the congregation was getting thrown off by the many pauses and places where they were stuck singing *a cappella* for long stretches. Finally, the song ended, with everyone silently staring at me.

Then, the whispers started while the octogenarian who'd been asked to offer the benediction hobbled with her walker up the long aisle to climb the stairs to the dais and the microphone.

Isn't that Hazel Hollings?

Why can't she play today?

Maybe the organ is broken.

Is she a stroke victim? I heard she had a tragic accident or incident. What happened? Does she need a doctor?

We love her so much—she's been our pride and joy. What can we do to help?

Did you happen to see the video footage of her injury?

I saw it. But I thought she was fine afterward.

I never heard anything. I'm so worried, too. I love her so much.

We all do. I wish I could just hug her and tell her we are proud of her no matter what.

Their caring kindness propelled me to my feet, and I stood beside the bench. Due to the curved choir balcony adding resonance to the space, the acoustics of the chapel made a microphone unnecessary for what I had to say.

"Thank you, everyone, for your kind and charitable reactions to my disastrous playing. I'm sorry I ruined matins." I sat down. But then I stood up again. "Maybe we can prevail upon a true musician to follow up by playing the postlude. Topanga Tycho is here, and she accompanied the candle-lighting service last night, as many of you know. Thank you for being so patient with me. I'm sorry for the mistakes. It won't happen again."

Just then, the elderly woman reached the stand. Her hearing aid chirped, and she adjusted it. "Let us pray."

She hadn't heard any of my speech. She just offered a beautiful Christmas prayer, and the service concluded.

Topanga did not, however, come up and take my spot on the bench. The congregants would be forced to leave the room sans musical accompaniment—another ruination of the Christmas matins, thanks to my hubris of thinking I could return to the public eye.

I grabbed a few tissues from atop the organ's box, and swabbed away the emotion. I even needed to blow my nose this time.

No one seemed to be leaving. They all stood in their spots in the pews as if waiting for something. They stared in the general direction of the organ.

One by one, they began waving to me, placing flat palms over their hearts, mouthing the words, "We love you," and a few even held up hearts made out of curved fingers and palms.

They weren't upset? They didn't want to run me out of town for wrecking their Christmas?

The song leader came over and patted my shoulder. "It's all right, Hazel. You don't need to pretend. Whatever happened wasn't your fault. Just keep being you, whether you play the organ or not."

Me? Still be me without playing music? Hard to imagine, but I thanked her. She leaned in and hugged me.

"I'm giving a proxy hug from all of us, sugar. We love you. Merry Christmas." She patted my shoulders and cheeks and then left the dais and headed out. The rest of the crowd, including the pastor and Ms. Eileen, moved out of the chapel, except for one person.

"Hazel?" Topanga climbed the steps with a plodding heaviness I'd never seen in her. "Do you have a minute? I need to talk to you."

What now? Was she going to mock me, tell me how much better an organist she was, cackle over winning Ike's affection? None of that seemed imminent from the look on her face, but she had fooled many people in the past. She came close, and we stood almost toe to toe on the small space between the organ bench and the choir seats.

"What is it, Topanga?" Resignation might have come through in my tone.

"First of all, I have a letter to deliver. Ms. Eileen cornered me before matins and made me promise to pass it along."

"She thinks you and I are friends?"

"No, she knew I had a reason to visit with you. Today." Topanga gave me the note.

I debated whether to open it right then or save it, but by reading it, I could postpone whatever freight train was coming down the tracks from my nemesis.

Hazel—

Forgive the old-fashioned note, but I'm up at Hobie's great white north hunting lodge and don't have other options for communication. Ms. Eileen probably gave you the original score I wrote for you this fall, but since then, my friend Ike got in contact with me and told me about the unfortunate situation with your hand. I don't have time to rescore my composition for you in time for this Christmas season, but I'll definitely have it ready for you by next fall so you can work it up in time for the holiday performances. I really hope you like it. I added lots of effects for the organ, including the bells. If you ever want a job doing composition consultations for me, I'd love some feedback from a true pro. Anyway, take care. Hope your hand heals up soon.

Love, Jesse Parrish

He'd offered to rewrite the composition especially for me? *At Ike's request?* I placed my useless hand over my mouth. What did it matter hiding it anymore? Everyone knew, even Topanga. Well, this all must have transpired *before* I told Ike to hit the road, but still—it was one of the nicest things anyone had ever done for me.

"You're crying." Topanga frowned.

"I know."

"You're always crying. Is something wrong with you?"

"Most definitely." I folded the note and stuck it in a pocket. "Thanks. Is that all?"

"I wish." Topanga rolled her eyes. "My dad and I had a terse conversation last night after Ike and I talked. There's something really important I need to tell you."

Chapter 18

Ike

Ipaced the snow-covered grounds of Falls View Chapel. Everyone seemed to have left matins, but Topanga hadn't come out yet. After all that yelling last night, I didn't much want to see her, but until she left, I didn't want to barge in on whatever she and Hazel were talking about.

Although, I had an idea.

Telling Topanga had been a massive betrayal of Hazel's confidence. Hazel had yet another reason to never forgive me, but I hoped she'd at least hear me out.

Wheels of a vehicle crunched on the gravel and snow, and a sports car parked at the close side of the church parking lot. "I hoped I might find you here." Out stepped Trey Tycho.

Blash. Hadn't the man received enough of an earful from me yesterday when I reamed him for his treatment of Hazel during her seizure? Why come back to the scene of the fight? Did he want to *actually* fight me? On Christmas morning?

"Mr. Tycho." I kept my voice flat. "Topanga is still inside."

"I had hoped so, and I'd wanted to run into you so we could talk privately."

"If you're going to file a suit against me for slander, go ahead. I didn't say anything that was untrue. Slander, by definition, must be false."

"There's no lawsuit. And I instructed my attorneys to drop

everything I'd had them cooking up against your girlfriend."

She wasn't my girlfriend anymore, but that point didn't matter right now. At least not to Tycho. Then again, it was the only thing that mattered to me.

"That's good to hear."

"What you said yesterday—it got me thinking. I appreciated your courage."

Um, thanks? But what was the point of saying so? "I don't usually get quite so strident."

"No, but it wasn't the only display of character. Your artwork itself showed bravery, the choice to stay true to your artistic vision, and to express it even when it went against the norms, while at the same time honoring the purpose of the piece. It impressed me. I would like to see your other works."

"Not until after things are made right with Hazel."

"I assumed you'd say that." He reached into his jacket's interior pocket. "That's why I dropped the lawsuit, arranged for a public apology to be made to her in person, and have cut this check to her for the remainder of her contract—plus an offer to pay for any medical bills she may incur when seeking treatment for her on-the-job injury. I consulted with a diagnostic specialist in Mendon. You know him, Dr. Cody Haught."

"I know him." I'd been in touch with him myself on the day Hazel and I went to Mendon to see Ms. Eileen in the hospital. "We were in medical school together." Cody had finished. I hadn't, and I had the debt to prove it.

"He said you'd already told him briefly about Hazel's situation and he'd researched several aspects of it and had some ideas by the time I showed up." Trey Tycho also explained what Cody had deduced after watching the link to the video of Hazel's devastating moment at the international concert that I'd sent him. "He has some ideas for treatment." Tycho cleared his throat. "I'd like to pay for any treatment he can recommend or give. He believes she can regain full use of her hand, in time, although he suspects the root cause might be something psychological." His brow got very dark. "If you think she'll allow it, again, I want to pay for all treatments. Until she's a hundred percent well."

It wasn't for me to say. "That's really big of you."

"I owe it to her and so much more." A frown pulled both edges of his mustache downward. "And I owe apologies to some other people, but what is Christmas for?" He took what looked like a bracing breath and then looked me straight in the eye again. "Thank you for the straight talk yesterday, and I'd like to work with you." He offered to shake on it. "If your other pieces are anything like the quality you created on the ceiling of Falls View Chapel, you and I are in for an amazing solo showing and sale to kick off the opening of my new gallery. What do you say?"

His hand hung in the air. Then dropped as I hesitated.

"You haven't seen my work."

"I expect to as soon as possible. Today's Christmas, so maybe tomorrow would be better. Your parents stopped me last night and told me there's a gathering today, and I assume you and Hazel will be obligated to attend that." He said some more things, but I fixated on the enormity of what had just happened.

"I would like to work with you if you agree that my artwork has the quality and value you expect in your choices for galleries."

"Values are going to be higher now that you've got a public exhibit on your list of accomplishments, believe me, especially one as well-received as that one." He aimed a thumb toward the chapel and named a large figure he expected one of my larger canvases could command.

Splutter, splutter, *what?* Just one sale alone would be enough to conquer the outstanding medical school bills—plus give me enough to actually pay rent for a few months.

Or buy Hazel a diamond ring.

We finally shook on it, and just then Topanga came out of the chapel and ran straight for her dad's sports car. She gave me a quick glance. Were those tears on her cheeks? Was Topanga even capable of crying?

"Goodbye, Ike. I'm looking forward to working with you." Trey slid into his car, and he and Topanga drove away.

To my shock, after the disaster that had seemed to belong to my future last night, I was looking forward to it, too.

Wow, Christmas really could be a time of miracles after all.

Would Hazel allow one for the two of us, too?

Chapter 19

Hazel

With the sun now streaming through the windows of the chapel and diffusing the winter light just so, I lay down on the front pew and studied Ike's creation while my mind swirled with the things Topanga had said—things I never could have imagined. Little streams of tears flowed from the edges of my eyes down my temples and into my hair. A sheer miracle had occurred—a healing one far more important than the one I'd needed for my right hand.

I looked heavenward, my heart full of thanks.

If only the healing could occur with Ike, too. But it was probably too late.

The back doors creaked open, and again, footfalls on wood filled the empty room. "Hazel?"

Ike's voice. I sat bolt-upright. "Ike? You came back? After the way I treated you, without even knowing what was going on, you shouldn't want to see me."

"I could never not want to see you." His face was soft, and his eyes were pleading. "Hazel, I have some information for you."

"Can it wait?" I launched myself into his arms. "You're not with Topanga." I showered his cheek with kisses. "You arranged for Jesse Parrish to create music I can play with just my left hand." I ran my fingers through his hair. "You told Topanga about my injury."

He pulled away. "I'm so sorry."

"No! It was the best thing that could've happened to us."

"Us, meaning …?"

"Meaning Topanga and me."

"Oh. How so?"

"She came to me after matins today. She said she and her dad had a stiff talk last night about how her mom had always compared her unfavorably to me, and that was why she'd tried sabotaging me for ages." Including the reason she'd sought Ike's attention in the first place years ago, but I left that part out. Her affection for him did grow in sincerity over time. Who could help it? Ike was so adorable. "She apologized for how she attacked me right before the international choir concert began that day."

"She attacked you?" Ike set me back by my shoulders and fury burned in those soulful eyes. "I'll—"

"No, no. Just with words."

"That's bad enough."

"She came to me with so much contrition just now, I can't hold it against her."

I didn't lay it all out for Ike, but Topanga had detailed the cruel way her mother held her up to me, and why she'd grown so bitter against me. When her mom left her dad this past summer, it had only grown worse, and she'd blamed me for all her problems, which made no sense. But she'd gone ballistic on me right before the concert, after receiving word that her mother had become engaged to someone new.

"You had a lot to do with it, though. The apology, I mean."

He angled his head. "Me?"

"You told her that she was an excellent musician and that her dad loved her no matter what."

"I did say that, but I also told her that I didn't want to have anything to do with her dad since he'd fired you right after your seizure."

"So it *was* a seizure?"

"That's what Cody Haught is convinced happened to cause your injury. A stress-induced psychosomatic injury."

That made some sense. "Ike, Topanga said she blamed herself for what you'd told her last night was a seizure—including her dad's cruel treatment of me."

Slowly, he nodded. "That makes sense. He cornered me outside a few minutes ago. He gave me this to pass to you." It was a small white envelope.

My heart skipped several beats as I opened it and took out a check. "That's the balance of my annual salary." I searched Ike's face.

"Yes, and he said more." Ike explained the content of his conversation with Trey Tycho, the promises that passed between them about me—and the potential deal between the two of them for placing Ike's artwork in Tycho's new Western Experience Gallery in Reedsville as a solo exhibition. "I really reamed him last night, so I had thought it was all over."

"You reamed Trey Tycho?"

"He badmouthed my girlfriend, hurting her when she was vulnerable. Do you think I'd let that stand if I had the chance to give him a hefty helping of the truth?"

"Oh, Ike!" I had to climb up on the seat of the pew to reach his mouth effectively with my own, but I kissed him with all the affection and contrition and hopes that exploded forth from my heart. "I am so in love with you."

"That's lucky," he said between kisses. "Because I happen to be in love with you, Hazel Hollings. Being with you is a blazing Christmas pudding set afire. It's a ride down a steep hill on a toboggan with brisk rushes of wind and snow crystals against my skin. It's the angels' songs and the sheer delight and wonder I felt in church as a boy. Will you"—he gave me a long, deep kiss—"be my girlfriend again?"

I kissed him one more time. "Only if we can renegotiate that status to something else soon."

"Very soon." He kissed me right there in the chapel, beneath the lost sheep being rescued and the morning sun and the star, for both my parents and all the rest of heaven to see. "Because I'm going to sell lots of paintings and buy us a little cottage on Society Row."

And live right here in Massey Falls? Well, why not?

Chapter 20

Hazel

"Can you help me pull this forward?" I hoisted my weight a little bit, and Ike helped me edge my bench closer to the keyboard. "It looks silly, I know, to be this pregnant and barely able to reach the keys."

"I'm sorry they didn't have a way to install an organ for the gallery." Ike perched on the edge of the bench beside me and helped me set up the music.

I placed my hands on the keys and began to play the song that was apparently always playing as the background music in my husband's mind: "Christmas With You." My dad's song. For me.

"It's all right," I said over the chords. "I'll just have to make do with this Steinway grand." Some sacrifice! "As long as my labor pains hold off, I'll make it through the grand opening. But your baby boy does seem to love it when I play this song. Is that why you requested it?"

Ike nuzzled my ear and whispered, "I fell in love with you when you played it for the first time while I was sketching for the ceiling artwork."

"That's not true." I lifted my hands from the keys, but kept down the sustain pedal. The baby stopped dancing in my belly. "You were in love with me long before that."

"I think I've loved you forever, Hazel. You're my forever. You and our son." He rested a hand on my belly. "My parents will be here any second. Let's keep you angled to the side and then give them the shock of their lives."

"They won't be shocked! We've been married since Valentine's Day."

"We eloped," he said. Only Aunt Gretchen had come as a witness, right before her permanent return to Massey Falls, where she'd taken a job teaching geography and world history at the high school. It was a good fit, and she was settling down at last.

"And you refused to inform them at the time. They had to find out through the grapevine." We'd discussed this often.

Not that I blamed Ike for keeping important things from them. They'd been such royal jerks to him that it was hard to trust them with the good things that happened these days. But now that he was a sought-after artist with a meteoric career trajectory, they had decided to show up in his life.

Lots of good things had shown up for both of us in the past year. Marriage, a baby on the way, Gretchen's permanent return to Massey Falls. For once, I wouldn't be alone at Christmas. Even Topanga might stop by during the holidays. She'd thrown me a baby shower, in fact. And now she was working for her dad as the organ accompanist for all his choirs in Reedsville. Funny how much a few months can change everything.

"Maybe it's time to let the past go," I said.

"I agree. And look to the future." He bent down and kissed my belly.

"Hey!" I ruffled his hair. "People are coming in." I pushed him off the bench to go greet guests and began playing "Christmas With You," which set our baby to kicking again.

Up walked Ike's favorite cousin, Calvin. "Buddy! You're putting down roots." He shot me a look. "And with a gorgeous girl. Now what am I going to do? My mom won't quit telling me I have to be more like my cousin Ike, the guy who makes commitments and follows his dreams." Calvin guffawed. "Could you stop being so darned perfect?

Just for me? For Christmas?"

They back-slapped, and Calvin went off to get refreshments and to flirt with Aunt Gretchen, it seemed from here. The charm streaming never stopped. I liked him—he'd been one of the only witnesses at our wedding.

Now and then, I looked up. Trey Tycho was welcoming everyone with a grin so wide his mustache had to stretch. And rightly so, since my gorgeous husband's art had netted Tycho a pretty penny. Or ten. The Western art craze had taken off last January, and the two of them had been a dozen steps ahead of the wave. And it didn't seem like it would crest or break anytime soon, considering the insane demand. Long before tonight's grand opening of the gallery, Tycho had placed every single piece of Ike's artwork from the storage unit onto the homes and office walls of hungry, high-paying collectors.

Luckily for all involved, Ike had honed his skill as a speed painter—as long as I played the background music for him. Goodness knew we needed the income so we could live in a home big enough to house a performance-sized electric organ, as well as his studio and a temperature-controlled storage area—plus plenty of room for a nursery.

What are we going to name him?

Between page turns, I kept my eye darting to the gallery doors. No sign of Ike's parents tonight yet. They might not come. Which would be a shame, as I'd sent them a special calligraphy-written invitation. *They'd better come with apologetic demeanors, too.*

Whoops—my chords hit crescendos a little aggressively just then, and heads swiveled toward the pianist, when they should be focused on the artist, not the music. My mistake. I chuckled a little, and the baby kicked once.

You're right, kiddo. Momma's gotta keep her emotions in check, and like Daddy says, focus on the future.

Just then, towering over all the heads of the patrons, Ike rushed toward the doors. There stood his parents, their frowns as pronounced as always. I left my spot and waddle-jogged to stand at his side. How

127

would Ike react? How would they?

Ike—was wonderful. As always. He embraced each of them, and then he gently took his mom by the arm. "Look, Mom. I want to show you this one especially. It might not seem like it unless you look closely, but I painted your father's face in that cowboy there." He led her a few steps to one of the largest canvases on display. "There's his chin-cleft. Can you spot it?"

Ike's dad glanced down at my stomach, disapprovingly. "I see you've been ..."

"I'm your daughter-in-law. Ike and I are expecting your grandson to arrive any day now. I'm glad you came so that you can congratulate Ike on his impending fatherhood."

"I thought you invited us so we could congratulate him on his choice to leave medicine, now that he's found so-called success." The guy's obstinance was as rock-solid as Mt. Rushmore.

So, it would be a while for that nut to crack.

And by nut, I did mean nut. "You're missing out, Dad." I might as well call him Dad. What did I have to lose? "There's joy to be had in forgiving people. Trust me, I know." I held up my right hand, which—after Topanga and I talked, and after Ike's friend Cody prescribed some physical therapy—had begun functioning again little by little throughout the year. "You probably heard about my injury. But when our baby is born—possibly tonight, in fact, based on this contraction I'm powering through right now—I'll be able to hold him with both my arms just fine. It's a miracle of forgiveness."

"But Isaac betrayed us." He narrowed his eyes at me. "Thanks to your dad."

"No, *my dad* believed in him and said so. Nothing more." And Ike had worn that belief like a shield, a breastplate of armor, for years—only retiring the sweater after we got married and I insisted. "I'm your daughter-in-law, Dad. Can you at least consider that you'd have a happier life if you decide Ike is still your son? Because I'm going to love you whether you like it or not." I swiped at my leaky eyes. They weren't actually leaking from emotion this time, believe it or not, but from the pain of the contraction.

Ooh, that was a strong one. Super strong. And following the last one by less than three minutes. "Ike?" I called. "I'm sorry—but can we?" I did those Lamaze breaths, fast and shallow. "Can we go to the hospital now?"

His mom was at my side in an instant. "A baby? You're having it now? Oh, sweetheart. Let's go! Honey, get her coat!" The woman pressed my lower back and steered me toward the exit. "Deano! Drop that fake *I'm mad at these kids* act this instant. We're going to be grandparents. Nothing else matters."

"But, Ike!" He was helping me into my coat, and I gripped his wrist. "Your exhibition." He began ushering me toward the car.

"There's nothing that can compete with this moment right now." He kissed my perspiring forehead. "Right, Mom and Dad?"

"Right!" his mom yelled.

Soon after, his dad grumbled. "Okay, you're right. Let's get this baby here safely—even if you're not going to be the doctor delivering him. What are you naming him?"

"We are thinking about calling him Dean," I said. "For his grandpa."

Ike looked down at me in amazement. "I thought you always said we'd call him Michelangelo—because we connected while I painted the chapel ceiling." He retrieved my hospital bag from our car and then placed me in the passenger scat of our SUV, and reached across to buckle me in. "And Sistine if we ever have a girl."

"Yeah, but can you picture him in Massey Falls Junior High when teacher calls roll on the first day when they always use people's full names? Even if his nickname is Mike or ... Angelo, he'd catch so much flak. We gotta consider his life at all points along the way and do the best we can by him."

"But we can still use Sistine when we have a girl?"

Part of me wanted to have *this* baby before deciding to have another. The contractions were about to knock me to the ground. "I love that you're planning future babies and a brimming household for us down the road." I loved the images of togetherness and full family love he always painted for us as time progressed. Those were his best artwork.

"You're a miracle," he whispered close to my ear. "A sheer gift from above."

"Get me to the hospital, please. I'm ready to meet little Dean."

And three hours of torture and—you guessed it—tears later, the nurses gave Ike his son.

"He's gorgeous," Ike breathed, gazing at him in amazement as he rested the baby in my arms.

We both looked at each other and laughed in happiness and relief. "Maybe we should call him Dean Isaac," I said.

"Why?" he asked, running a fingertip across his little wrinkled, red forehead.

"Because don't you know? Isaac means laughter. And you helped me to laugh again, and I have a strong sense that we're going to have many days of laughter and joy with this one."

"Stop it! Your salty tears are dripping on his cheek!" Ike kissed our baby, and then he tilted my chin up and kissed me too, and in it I saw my whole future of joy roll out like the harmonious chords of an organ with the swell pedal fully open.

Epilogue

Amanda Starkey

"Amanda Starkey, please come to the third floor." The work intercom system paged me for the fifth time, even though I was already in the elevator and about to pop out of my snow boots. "Amanda Starkey, third floor to meet Ms. Grimes, please."

If only Bessemer would cooperate, I would absolutely get there, and fast. For the hundredth time, I punched that third-floor button, but his doors would *not* close.

"Come on, Bessemer. Please? It's for my big chance on the creative team."

Okay, not actually for my big chance *this time*, since all I was doing today was delivering the same old layouts. But, if I showed Georgia and the other executives I was reliable and competent, they'd agree to give my request to be on the Belgian Bliss Candies creative team serious consideration. Right? "Please, Bessemer? For me?"

Christmas *muzak* piped through Winters Plaza's speakers—a weird, synthesizer version of "Jingle Bells," chosen by someone devoid of any traditional Christmas respect. I raised a fist to the ceiling speakers and—*what was that?*

"Who put mistletoe in Bessemer?" I called out into the empty hallway of the sub-subbasement. A sprig of velvety sage green leaves and white berries stuck out from between the panels of the ceiling. He would not like that. In fact, he was probably offended and therefore not willing to move.

With soothing tones, I patted the wall panel and coaxed Bessemer. "You know I'd never leave you or Winters Plaza if it were up to me." The building was far too embedded in Reedsville's historic roots, too architecturally gorgeous, to dream of moving. I'd be crushed when we came back from the hiatus relocated somewhere with lots of steel and glass instead. Even if being somewhere new included my own small office with a door and an elevator without personality quirks.

As if assuaged by my reassurances, Bessemer lurched like Santa's sleigh being jerked by harnessed reindeer. He hiccuped. He jarred. His doors might even close.

Please move—please-oh-please-oh-please.

Maybe I should take the stairs. It was only fifteen flights. I could do it, even with the heavy pile of folios with prepared layouts that I'd leaned against Bessemer's side wall. Fifteen flights was nothing, right?

But at top speed? I was not in that type of shape. And arriving out of breath would make Georgia look at me askance. It had happened in the past.

But when Bessemer still didn't move, what choice did I have? "You're forcing me to give up on you, pal." I took a step to get off and head toward the stairwell. I hoisted my folio, and—of course, Bessemer's doors screeched and lurched an inch, another, and another toward closing.

"*Yes.* Thank you, Bessemer." I set down my folio and patted his wall. This was it. A low buzzing filled the air, as if a call to adventure mixed into this elevator trip to the third floor.

Or ... not. Because—

"Hold the door please." A hand shot into the breach, and Bessemer's sensors retracted his doors. The man I least wanted to see in the world stepped confidently onto the elevator. "Hey, Mandy. How you doing? Have you been talking out loud to the elevator?"

"Calvin! How could you?" I could've twisted Calvin Turner's hand right off. And not just because he was making me late for my third-floor page-a-thon. "Bessemer was finally starting to move after sitting here offended and stubborn for three minutes."

No way was I going to point out the mistletoe as the source of offense. Not to Calvin Turner, the financial consultant every woman in SolutionX was panting after, even though he had the reputation of being a serial make-out artist. The *kiss 'em and diss 'em* guy who loped through the second subbasement floor three times a week, picking up a new girl's phone number each time.

Well, not mine. Not ever.

Calvin petted the brass wall. "Bessie's like an old mare. You have to know how to finesse her." His perfect hair and his never-rumpled electric blue suit stepped in front of the panel. "There, there, sweetheart. Take us where we need to go, please." He spoke softly, almost sexily, his lips a quarter inch from the numerical floor buttons.

"You're gross. And Bessemer is a *he*, not a *she*."

"I'm not gross. I know how to get what I want."

Unfortunately, that might've been true. According to rumors, Calvin Turner had sowed so many wild oats he could've qualified for a farm loan. Every woman on my floor had gone out with him at some point or other over the past year.

Make that, every woman except me.

Of course, I was way too smart to fall for that whole façade. The chiseled mass of baseless confidence that strolled like clockwork past my cubicle on his way to the water cooler between appointments held no fascination for me.

Well, not much anyway.

"How's your hobbit crush doing? Is he even considering getting his feet waxed? Because hairy feet are so last year."

Oh, yes, don't forget the other reason his glow dimmed in my eyes: he also peppered me with torments about the motivational picture on the wall beside my desk as he passed. Lord of the Rings had depth and wisdom and adventure. Who in their right mind didn't like that?

Oh, that was it—Calvin must never be in his right mind.

"Thanks for the fashion trend tip. I'll get him a gift certificate to the salon and put it in his Christmas stocking."

He raised one brow in a sultry gaze. "What are you going to put in my Christmas stocking?" The charm flowed from him like molasses and honey—filled with ants, gasping for their lives.

"My foot, most likely." I could've kicked his shin. The guy was such a jerk about the motivational poster near my desk. Photo only, no words, but just the picture conjured profound feelings, so no words were needed.

He wouldn't understand.

"Quit breathing on the other floors' buttons, would you? Don't you know about Bessemer's fatal quirk? If you even hover a finger over the button, the elevator will sense it. I have to get to seven. So, hold that steamy breath and back away from the panel."

"She's highly sensitive to touch?" There was flirtation in Calvin's eye—for the first time ever directed at me. "And you're calling my breath *steamy*?"

"Absolutely bursting with hot air."

He waved his hand near the buttons, threatening to light up every one of them. Bessemer's muzak station started playing "The Twelve Days of Christmas," its manic repetition the perfect mirror of my mood.

"Please, Calvin!" I lunged for him, and just then, the doors shut. "Oh, hallelujah."

"You're thanking me. Nice. You're welcome. Is there anything else I can do for you this holiday season, Amanda?"

So, he knew my actual name. I wasn't Mandy or Hobbit Girl to him? Stop. The. Presses. Was Calvin actually flirting with me? *Me?* The girl he'd systematically ignored all year? Okay, so maybe I'd been a little ego-bruised while he lavished all the other women with compliments and only teased me about Frodo Baggins.

"Yes, as a matter of fact. You can press seven." Bessemer's floor-button lights had all blinked off again. "Never mind. I'm just going up the stairwell."

"You can't. Its closed."

"They can't do that. It's against fire code."

"There are exterior fire escapes."

That meant Bessemer was my only option for getting to the third floor? I was doomed. "I'm going to call Georgia Grimes and explain why I'm late." And kiss my chance at the creative team goodbye. She'd think I was unreliable or incompetent. I hadn't even dared show her my artwork yet. I'd been saving it for the big moment when an exec took notice of me.

"Here's another gift. Merry Christmas," he said. And then ... he pressed two. For the second floor.

I cringe-screamed. "Why are you being so stupid?"

"I'm not stupid."

"Wanna make a bet?" I muttered.

On the word *bet*, Calvin's eyes caught fire. He shot me the world's most flirtatious look. It did something wacky to my belly—worse than any lurchy ride up or down in Bessemer's cabin. "If there's one thing I can never resist, it's a bet."

Oh, brother. Spare me this moment. "Never mind. Pretend I didn't say that."

"What type of bet?" He was still flirting with the panel. Dimwit.

"Don't you hear them paging me nonstop?"

"They're kinda relentless, aren't they."

I dialed Lisa on my phone. It was dead.

"There's no cell signal in Bessemer. Her walls are a foot thick, solid steel."

"That's not even science." And Bessemer was a him, not a her.

"Maybe not, but that doesn't change the fact that Bessemer is a cell-phone dead zone." He smiled. "You're stuck here. All alone with me." He stepped a little closer. "Do you know what this reminds me of? Those games in junior high where you go into the closet with someone. Seven minutes in heaven."

My face went hotter than roasting chestnuts on an open fire. "Have you ever heard of workplace sexual harassment?"

"Yes, and I'd love lessons in it."

"Calvin!"

"I'm just kidding." He held up both palms and backed away from the panel. "It's just, you're—" A gleam lit his eye. "What will you give me?"

"An iota of respect?" Bessemer creaked. He might move at last! "Come on. It's finally ready to move. Don't tempt fate."

"You're saying fate is all around us, Amanda Starkey?" He placed a hand against the wall and leaned over me, a look in his eye smoldering as if he thought he was too good-looking to be resisted. "And that I'm tempting?"

"What you are is insufferable." *And tempting.*

At that moment, Bessemer jerked upward. Movement! Soon they could stop paging me for the folio layouts I'd formatted and printed, staying late last night because the hardest job to do is the one you never start, or so says the wisdom of the hobbits.

"Even if you're not tempted, Bessie will succumb to my charms." He waved his other hand much too close to the fourth-floor button.

No!

"Knock it off." I ducked beneath his arm and stood between him and the panel—and much too close to Calvin's smolder. "Ahem. I have to get to the third floor sometime this week."

He leaned nearer. Our noses practically touched. He smelled better than he looked, and he looked too good to be true. Which, duh, he was. Totally. Everything about Calvin Turner was an act. Big hat, no cattle.

If he'd been employed directly by SolutionX, rather than just acting as a consultant, he would've been their finest show-pony.

Whereas, I was their workhorse.

Workhorse status meant they'd never recognized my potential as a creative contributor—at least not yet. This meeting on the third floor could open doors for me, creatively.

"What's the fire to get upstairs, Starkey? You think your hairy-footed true love is waiting for you up there?" His breath feathered past my cheek.

I closed my eyes to shut out the intensity of Calvin's gaze. "Let's leave the hobbits out of this. What did they ever do to you?"

"Oh, lots. By being plastered to your cubicle wall, they kept your attention off me, for instance."

"Does every woman have to fall at your feet for you to be happy? Is that it?" A Tolkien quote about potatoes came to mind, but I applied it to Calvin: *boil 'im, mash 'im, stick 'im in a stew.* "All the girls on the second subbasement floor have been through your revolving door. Isn't that enough?"

A frown flickered across his face. "Not all the girls on the second subbasement floor." He inched his face a little closer to mine.

I swallowed hard. Why was my body chemistry reacting to this ... play-actor? I would've moved out of his path but I was guarding the panel.

Bessemer clunked to a halt. "Finally. I'm getting off here."

"Between floors two and three?"

What? I jerked my head upward, and the dial pointed—sure enough—between the two floors. "This is your fault." I whipped my face back toward Calvin, who still stood over me, when—"Ouch." Something tugged mightily at my ponytail.

"I think you're stuck." Calvin moved his arm, which pulled my hair even harder.

"Don't you mean *we're* stuck? Between floors?"

"Yep, and your—whatever that thing is in your hair—horsefly swatter?"

"My ponytail?" Ouch. It stung when yanked.

"Whatever. It's stuck on the buttons of my jacket." He edged into my personal space and put his other arm around my neck, working his wrist near the back of my head.

I'd never been this close to Calvin Turner. Never wanted to be. Unless that recurring dream counted—the one where he got too close and I woke up in a cold sweat. But my *conscious* self had never wanted Calvin this near to me.

"It's really stuck." He pulled me closer, his hands moving behind me slowly, almost a caress. "Hang on there, Mandy."

"Uh-huh," I said in a reflexive swoon. Apparently, my hormones were on board with Dream-life Amanda, instead of Conscious Daytime Amanda. Chances were, after a long winter's nap they were buzzing to life with his nearness. The clean shave, the ridge of his jaw line, the dark lashes fringing his blue eyes all were near enough to kiss collectively and individually.

Kiss? No! I would not be kissing any portion of Calvin Turner.

Bessemer lurched upward. I thrust my arms around Calvin's torso for balance. "Whoa, Bessemer!"

"Whoa, Amanda." His smolder deepened into glowing embers.

Great. I was now embracing Calvin Turner, consummate player, and chewing out an elevator at the same time.

My life had come to this.

Calvin's phone chimed a text. He left off working on my hair and reached into his jacket pocket with his free hand.

It's not that I'm sneaky, it's that he held it where I couldn't help but see.

Are you bringing a Serious Girlfriend to my wedding, or are you losing our bet?

Bonus Recipe: Aunt Elly's Norwegian Krumkake

My great-aunt Elly was the first child in her family born in the United States after they immigrated from Norway. She and her sisters (including my grandma) preserved many of their Norwegian traditions, including some delicious recipes. One of the favorites is *krumkake*, a waffle cookie made with an iron, turned on a dowel into a conical shape, and loaded with butter and cardamom. The irons are available for sale online for a reasonable price, but the cookies themselves and the memories they represent are priceless. Aunt Elly's recipe is transcribed below, with her special notes included.

Ingredients:

1 ¼ c butter or margarine

2 ½ c flour

1 ¼ c sugar

2 eggs

1 tsp cardamom

¼ tsp salt

1 c water

Instructions:

Cream eggs and butter. Add sugar. Cream together well. Add half of the flour and beat in well. Add remaining flour, cardamom, and salt. Mix, and slowly add water. I don't use the whole thing, just as much as needed to create a batter-dough consistency. Bake on krumkake iron until golden. Roll on cone immediately and cool. Can be served with a mixture of half Cool Whip, half strawberry jam.

Author's Notes

Thank you for reading *Candlelight Chapel*. Though the premise of a psychosomatic response to a traumatic event may seem far-fetched as the basis for this story, I actually experienced right-hand paralysis myself. It was the fall of 2020, within a few days of learning that my dear, loving mother *and* my closest friend of over twenty years both had been diagnosed with terminal stomach cancer.

I mentioned the situation to my wonderful readers, and they gave me suggestions for carpal tunnel, which I tried, but in my heart, I knew that it was due to heartache, not overuse.

Eventually, with Heaven's grace, my hand returned to usefulness. That challenging time gave me the inspiration for Hazel's conflict in this story because I knew how real it could be and how healing—on an emotional level—can bring physical restoration.

And so, it's no coincidence that this (outwardly secular) story takes place in a chapel.

The title of the story came to me first, as is often my process, but once I envisioned the Falls View Chapel, I knew exactly what experiences could take place there, and how love could be the balm for both broken characters. Many readers had commented to me that their favorite holiday tradition is attending a candle-lighting service. Thank you for this wonderful idea, if you're one who shared the very inspiring imagery with me.

And thank you so much for being a reader of my books.

In addition, I had intended to add details about the organ that Hazel

Hollings plays. The Falls View Chapel would have had an electric organ, but the organ is an instrument of ancient date, and can be powered by bellows or electricity. I researched many things about the organ. I apologize for not filling the story chock-full of those interesting details to make her skills authentic. However, it became clear that my enthusiasm for the details and geeking out would distract from the story itself. But I do love hearing the organ played, especially in chapels at Christmastime.

Acknowledgments

Thank you to Bruce Griffith for sharing his writing space with me and for always being a wonderful, supportive father-in-law. I married into the best family.

Thank you to Mary Mintz and Paula Bothwell for editing expertise, to the readers of my light fiction for their support and ideas—especially for their love of Christmas and suggestion for a candle-lighting service as a backdrop for a novel.

Many thanks to my husband for being my muse and alpha reader (there's nothing beta about him). He is always the hero of the romance story.

And as always, my thanks is to God for the gift of creation and the opportunity to write.

A Note from the Author about the Series

All books in this series of clean Christmas romances celebrate family, tradition, Christmas, belief, and love. They're available in ebook, paperback, hardcover, and in audio.

Each is a **standalone romance**, but they do connect in the small-town world and can be best enjoyed in a "loop."

For example, book 1 leads to book 2, and so on, and at the end, book 10 loops back to book 1, with recurring characters. In other words, a reader can **start with any book**, read the subsequent book, and then complete the loop.

Thank you for reading, and I hope you enjoy all the books, as well as any of my other Christmas-centered stories, many which are found in the Sugarplum Falls Romances and the Snowfall Wishes series.

Sending you greetings of Christmas cheer all year long.

The Christmas House Romance Series

The Christmas Cookie House
The Sleigh Bells Chalet
The Holiday Hunting Lodge
Peppermint Drop Inn
The Candy Cane Cottage
The Hot Chocolate Shop
Starlight Haven
The Candlelight Chapel
The Mistletoe Lift
Yuletide Manor

About the Author

Jennifer Griffith is the *USA Today* bestselling author of over fifty novels and novellas. Two of her novels have received the Swoony Award for best secular romance novel of the year. She lives in Arizona with her husband, who is a judge and her muse. They are the parents of five brilliant children.

Connect with Jennifer at authorjennifergriffith.com, where you can sign up for her newsletter to receive exclusive content and notices of new releases.

Made in United States
Troutdale, OR
12/10/2024